A VERY NAUGHTY ANGEL

Barbara Cartland

Barbara Cartland Ebooks Ltd

This edition © 2014

SO-CEX-976

Book design by M-Y Books

m-ybooks.co.uk

The Barbara Cartland
Eternal Collection

The Barbara Cartland Eternal Collection is the unique opportunity to collect all five hundred of the timeless beautiful romantic novels written by the world's most celebrated and enduring romantic author.

Named the Eternal Collection because Barbara's inspiring stories of pure love, just the same as love itself, the books will be published on the internet at the rate of four titles per month until all five hundred are available.

The Eternal Collection, classic pure romance available worldwide for all time .

THE LATE DAME BARBARA CARTLAND

Barbara Cartland, who sadly died in May 2000 at the grand age of ninety eight, remains one of the world's most famous romantic novelists. With worldwide sales of over one billion, her outstanding 723 books have been translated into thirty six different languages, to be enjoyed by readers of romance globally.

Writing her first book 'Jigsaw' at the age of 21, Barbara became an immediate bestseller. Building upon this initial success, she wrote continuously throughout her life, producing bestsellers for an astonishing 76 years. In addition to Barbara Cartland's legion of fans in the UK and across Europe, her books have always been immensely popular in the USA. In 1976 she achieved the unprecedented feat of having books at numbers 1 & 2 in the prestigious B. Dalton Bookseller bestsellers list.

Although she is often referred to as the 'Queen of Romance', Barbara Cartland also wrote several historical biographies, six autobiographies and numerous theatrical plays as well as books on life, love, health and cookery. Becoming one of Britain's most popular media personalities and dressed in her trademark pink, Barbara spoke on radio and television about social and political issues, as well as making many public appearances.

In 1991 she became a Dame of the Order of the British Empire for her contribution to literature and her work for humanitarian and charitable causes.

Known for her glamour, style, and vitality Barbara Cartland became a legend in her own lifetime. Best remembered for her wonderful romantic novels and loved by millions of readers worldwide, her books remain treasured for their heroic heroes, plucky heroines and traditional values. But above all, it was Barbara Cartland's overriding belief in the positive power of love to help, heal and improve the quality of life for everyone that made her truly unique.

AUTHOR'S NOTE

Obernia is a fictitious country but the Linderhof when I visited it some year ago was as mystical, exciting and beautiful as Tilda found it.

For the purpose of my story I have made Munich a little nearer to King Ludwig's dream Palace than it is in actual fact.

CHAPTER ONE
1879

The train puffed slowly into Windsor.

Although the station was not cleared as it was when Queen Victoria travelled, there were several resplendent officials in lavishly gold-braided uniforms to meet the Princess Priscilla, Duchess of Forthampton, and her daughter.

A Royal carriage was waiting outside the station, the ladies were helped into it and they drove off towards Windsor Castle.

"Do remember, Tilda," Princess Priscilla said, "that you do *not* speak to the Queen until she speaks to you."

"Yes, Mama."

"And remember, take Her Majesty's hand, curtsey right to the ground, then kiss her hand and afterwards her cheek."

"Yes, Mama."

"And listen attentively, Tilda, to everything she says."

"Yes, Mama."

"Promise me, Tilda, that you will not ask questions. You are far too fond of asking questions. I have told you that before."

"How can one learn the answers, Mama, unless one asks the questions?"

"That is the sort of comment I would expect you to make. Oh, dear, I wish your Papa could have come with us! I feel you always behave in a more circumspect manner when he is present."

There was no answer.

Lady Victoria Matilda Tetherton-Smythe had heard her mother say all these things not once but hundreds of times since the invitation to Windsor Castle had arrived.

She had learnt from long experience that it was much the best policy to agree to everything anyone said to her and to let her thoughts follow their own course.

She was thrilled at the thought of seeing Windsor Castle and she craned her neck to peep through the carriage windows.

At the moment, however, there were only houses to be seen on either side of them and she had not yet had a glimpse of the massive structure whose history had excited her imagination.

Her teachers had taught her that Windsor Castle had been built first by William I.

He had been attracted by the position of a steep hill high above a river so that a subject and unfriendly people could constantly be reminded of their intimidating Norman conquerors.

'They must have hated him!' Tilda said to herself.

"You are not attending to me, Tilda!" her mother said. "What did I say?"

"I am sorry, Mama, I was thinking of something else."

"You are always thinking of something else!" Princess Priscilla snapped. "Do listen, Tilda."

"I am listening, Mama."

"I told you to remember that from now on you will be called 'Victoria' by everyone. You were christened after the Queen and it was obvious that that was what you must be called as she was your Godmother."

"I hate the name Victoria!" Tilda replied.

"Your father does not like it either," Princess Priscilla said, "which was why we started to call you 'Matilda'. Of course it became abbreviated to the rather common 'Tilda'."

"I like it, Mama."

"Your likes and dislikes are not of the slightest consequence. Til – I mean, Victoria."

"It's no use, Mama," Tilda smiled, "you will never remember to call me Victoria, whatever they may do in Obernia."

"You will certainly be Victoria to the Obernians," Princess Priscilla replied, "and, Tilda, do remember that the Queen herself has arranged your marriage."

"I have not forgotten, Mama."

"It is a great honour. You should be very proud."

Tilda did not answer and after a moment her mother went on,

"Not many girls of your age have the chance of being the reigning Princess over a country of some considerable importance in Europe."

"It is a long way – away," Tilda murmured.

She would have said more, but at that moment she had a view of Windsor Castle and she found that it was just as impressive and splendid as she had expected it would be.

She found herself thinking of the Knights of old who had taken part in jousting tournaments.

She could almost imagine that she could see them with their specially painted shields and richly embroidered saddles and swords whose pummels and hilts were gilded with pure gold.

'I wish I could have been here then,' Tilda thought.

Each Knight had a fair lady whom he esteemed as a paragon of beauty and to whom he paid his vows and addressed himself on the day when the mock battles proved both his gallantry and his manhood.

The horses were climbing the steep incline up to The Castle door and Tilda found herself thinking that she was following the route taken so often by Queen Elizabeth.

How magnificent she had been with her fragile figure and her strong will, her graciousness and her robust beer-drinking.

She had liked to hunt in the Park and was capable of killing a 'great and fat stag with her own hand'.

Everyone had acclaimed her majesty and her greatness, and yet she had never married.

'Perhaps she did not wish to have a husband chosen for her,' Tilda thought to herself.

The carriage came to a stop outside the front door.

"Now remember, Tilda, everything I have told you," Princess Priscilla said in an agitated tone. "The Queen has not seen you for years. You must make a good impression on her."

"I will do my best, Mama."

They walked into the fourteenth century Gothic entrance hall and moved along the passages, which seemed dark but had, Tilda recognised, richly carved cornices and frames by Grinling Gibbons.

She did not know why, but his carvings always excited her.

The leaves, the fruit, the fish and game had a graceful symmetry and at the same time they seemed to evoke some personal response that she could not understand.

She always felt the same about anything that was very beautiful and it was a feeling of excitement deep inside herself.

On they went led by a solemn-faced Major Domo and Tilda knew that her mother was feeling nervous.

Princess Priscilla had a habit of drawing in her lips and pressing them together when she was agitated.

She also fidgeted with her scarf, her handbag and the front of her gown.

'It's all right, Mama. The Queen cannot eat you!' Tilda longed to say.

But she knew that such a remark would only upset her mother even more than she was already.

It was, she had learnt, surprising that the Queen should be at Windsor.

For years she had refused to leave Osborne where she preferred to be and where she had stayed in seclusion unseen by the public since the Prince Consort's death.

But the political events of last year and the tense situation with Russia had brought her a new vitality and what her statesmen averred was a rejuvenation.

It was difficult for them to understand that the perpetual strain of the political situation and its constant calls on her judgement were precisely the tonic she needed.

Hitherto Her Majesty had wailed and protested at the cruel way in which she was overworked, at the callousness of those who teased and tormented her to make exertions she was incapable of.

She had been full of self-pity for the lonely lot of the 'poor Queen', but now there was an end to that.

Instead of insisting on remaining at Osborne or fleeing to Balmoral in Scotland to the great inconvenience of the members of the Government, she had moved into Windsor Castle.

Instead of having to be urged by her Ministers to greater activity, it was now she who hustled and spurred them on.

No doubt the fact that she was working with Mr. Benjamin Disraeli, a Prime Minister whom she liked and trusted, was one very important reason for the change.

As Mr. Disraeli himself put it later,

"She gave her Prime Minister inspiration and he gave her devotion!"

Whatever the reasons, it was a considerable convenience for Statesmen, politicians and relations to have the Queen at Windsor.

Coming down on the train Princess Priscilla had said to her daughter,

"It is a wearisome journey to Osborne and I should have hated to leave your Papa for so long."

The Duke of Forthampton, who had been uniquely honoured in being allowed, as a commoner, to marry a Royal Princess and a great-niece of the Queen, was in ill health.

Doubtless the distinction he had been accorded in marriage was due to the fact that he was one of the richest men in England.

Yet, while the marriage had been arranged, it had undoubtedly, from everybody's point of view, been a success.

The only tragedy was that as the Duke was considerably older than his wife – and there might have been other reasons as well – there had been only one child of the marriage, Victoria Matilda.

This meant that regrettably there was no direct heir to the Dukedom.

It was a surprise when the Queen remembered her Godchild when she was furthering her matchmaking plans for the eligible crowned heads of Europe.

"How like Great-Aunt Victoria!" Princess Priscilla had exclaimed to her husband when they received a letter informing them that the Queen was arranging for Victoria Matilda to become the wife of Prince Maximilian of Obernia.

"What do you mean by that?" the Duke enquired.

"I thought the Queen had completely forgotten Tilda's existence," Princess Priscilla answered. "Last time we were at Osborne she never even referred to her and now out of the blue she arranges her marriage."

"It is an honour, my dear," the Duke remarked.

Princess Priscilla sighed.

"I only hope that Tilda will think so too."

Tilda, as it happened had taken the news with some surprise, but she did not protest as her mother had half-feared she might.

Tilda was always unpredictable.

What her mother did not realise was that Tilda at the age of eighteen was finding the Forthampton estate in Worcestershire where she was incarcerated year after year exceedingly dull.

It was not that she did not have plenty to occupy her mind. There were Governesses, Tutors, hobbies and crafts in which she interested herself.

She also liked riding and, although she was not allowed to hunt, her father had given her two horses of her own which were spirited, quite unlike the quiet lazy animals that most girls of her age were mounted upon.

Because of the Duke of Forthampton's arthritis, which almost completely crippled him, there was no suggestion that Tilda should take part in the London Season or have a ball given for her debut as she might have expected.

She was, it is true, taken to London to be presented and to make her curtsey in the Throne Room at Buckingham Palace.

The Queen had been present during the first hour before she handed over such an arduous duty to her son, the Prince of Wales and his beautiful Danish wife, Alexandra.

Tilda had made her curtsey amongst the first group of Royals, after which she had found the proceedings over-formal and just as boring as she had expected.

It seemed to her that people spoke in a different voice to Royalty from that which they used to more ordinary folk.

Because her mother came into the first category, there was no doubt that conversation with those who approached the Princess was stilted and not particularly interesting.

*

The Major Domo leading them through The Castle now paused.

They had reached the Queen's apartments and, after a short wait, they were shown into the drawing room where the Queen was seated in an armchair, the table beside her covered with a fringed cloth.

In her shapeless but expensive black satin dress, shining black boots with elastic tops and widow's cap, she looked, as Tilda had expected, old and rather awe-inspiring.

It was difficult to realise that this little woman was the ruler of an immense Empire and that practically every Monarch in Europe was related to her.

Princess Priscilla had told her daughter that the four rooms the Queen used contained almost two hundred pictures as well as many photographs of her relations.

They were carried from Windsor to Balmoral or Osborne every time she moved.

Tilda saw them now on a desk and on tables by the heavy damask curtains of crimson red.

They stood amongst a profusion of bundles of letters, sheets of music, paperweights, inkstands, old penknives and the 'Queen's Birthday Book'.

This was full of the signatures of her visitors, which she took with her wherever she went, so that it was sometimes mistaken for a Bible.

It was difficult for Tilda to take in many details of the room or indeed of the Queen herself, for she was trying to remember all the instructions her mother had given her.

The Princess was already in front of Her Majesty sweeping down to the ground in a deep curtsey and then rising to kiss the Queen's hand and then her cheek.

"So this is Victoria!"

The voice sounded unexpectedly high.

The Queen's eyes were perceptive and searching as Tilda curtseyed as she had been instructed to do, touching the pale soft cheek with her lips, then kissing the blue-veined hand.

"Yes, this is Victoria, ma'am," Princess Priscilla said a little breathlessly.

"I want to talk to you, Victoria!"

"Yes, ma'am."

Tilda thought that whenever people said that they wanted to talk to you, it usually meant they were going to scold or tell you something unpleasant, but the Queen continued,

"Your mother will have told you that you are to marry Prince Maximilian of Obernia?"

"Yes, ma'am."

"It is a position of great importance for several reasons."

"Yes, ma'am."

"The first is because I consider Prince Maximilian worthy of having an English bride and someone who is one of my relatives."

"I am sure he esteems it a great honour, ma'am," Princess Priscilla interposed.

The Queen did not take her eyes from Tilda's face.

"The second reason," she went on as if the Princess had not spoken, "Is that Obernia occupies a very important place in our political strategy concerning Europe."

Tilda raised her blue eyes to the Queen's.

This, she thought, was quite interesting.

"You must understand," Queen Victoria went on, "that Obernia, as it borders on Bavaria, Austria and Wurttemberg, is a very significant factor in the balance of power in that it remains independent."

The Queen paused, but did not seem to expect a reply and went on,

"Prussia, by making William Emperor and swallowing up many of the smaller states, has created a situation of which we are somewhat apprehensive."

The Queen's voice was sharp and there was no doubt at all that her disapproval was strong.

The Princess knew it was not only the transformation of the former German Federation into an Empire that was upsetting the Queen, but the behaviour of her grandson, Prince William of Prussia.

All the family knew that Willy's pride, fostered by Bismarck and his grandparents, was making him intolerably arrogant.

The Queen had been informed that he even listened with approval to insulting remarks about his English mother, her eldest daughter Vicky.

"Why Bavaria ever agreed in the first place to Prince Bismarck's proposals, I shall never know!" the Queen went on as if speaking to herself.

"I have always heard, ma'am," Princess Priscilla said, "that it was because King Ludwig had toothache! "

It had been suggested that a Prussian or a Bavarian Monarch might rule either jointly or alternately over the German Federation, but the King of Bavaria, rather than argue on such a vital point when he was in pain, conceded the position to Prussia.

"I am aware of the circumstances in which this regrettable decision was made," the Queen said crushingly.

Princess Priscilla flushed.

"Whatever happened eight years ago, the fact remains," the Queen continued, "that Bavaria is now part of the German Federation, although I believe King Ludwig is allowed more licence than the other members."

She paused to say emphatically,

"What is obvious is that Obernia must at all costs remain independent."

Her Majesty now switched her attention from Princess Priscilla.

"Do you understand, Victoria?" she asked. "You will, in an indirect capacity, be an Ambassador for England. You must influence your husband to realise that co-operation with us rather than with Germany will be always to his advantage."

The Queen spoke forcefully and then, looking at her Godchild, she said unexpectedly,

"You look very young!"

Her Majesty was speaking nothing but the truth for Tilda in fact appeared to be hardly more than a child.

Small and slight with fair hair the colour of spring sunshine and china-blue eyes which seemed to fill her little flower-like face, she looked absurdly immature, far too young to be married.

"Victoria is eighteen, ma'am," Princess Priscilla said nervously.

"That is the age I became Queen and I also looked young."

"Were you frightened, ma'am, when you were told you were to be Queen?" Tilda asked.

Princess Priscilla drew in her breath.

This was just the type of question that she had warned her daughter against making, for it was a presumption that would undoubtedly annoy the Queen.

To her surprise, however, after a pause the Queen answered,

"It was frightening when I was awoken at six o'clock in the morning by my Mama to be told that the Archbishop of Canterbury and Lord Conyngham wished to see me."

"That must have been a surprise!" Tilda murmured.

Her eyes were on the Queen and they were full of interest.

"I got out of bed," the Queen went on, "and went into my sitting room alone wearing only my dressing gown. Lord Conyngham, the Lord Chamberlain, then acquainted me with the fact that my poor uncle, the King, was no more and consequently I was the Queen."

Tilda drew in her breath.

"It must have been a shock, ma'am!"

"It was!" the Queen answered, "but I was determined that I would be good!"

As if suddenly she realised that she had been almost too familiar in her reminiscing she added sharply,

"And that is what you must be, Victoria – *good!* And always loyal to your country. Remember whatever name you have, however important your position, there is English blood – *my blood* – running through your veins!"

"I will remember, ma'am."

There was little more conversation before Princess Priscilla and Tilda were dismissed from the Royal presence.

They partook of a light meal with two of the Queen's Ladies-in-Waiting before the carriage carried them to the station and they were once again on the train travelling back to London.

"Well, that is over!" Princess Priscilla exclaimed.

She settled herself comfortably in the corner of their reserved carriage and let out a sigh of relief.

"You are scared of her, Mama," Tilda said. "I cannot think why."

"Everyone is frightened of her," Princess Priscilla answered. "You were lucky. She was charming to you. She can be very awe-inspiring."

"That is what a Queen should be," Tilda said, then laughed, "but I doubt, Mama, if anyone would be scared of me!"

"You will not be a Queen, Tilda, only a reigning Princess," Princess Priscilla corrected. "Although I cannot understand why with so many Kings and Grand Dukes in Europe, Obernia has never had a King."

"I expect it is too small," Tilda suggested.

"You sound very disparaging about the country that is soon to be yours," Princess Priscilla remarked reprovingly.

"It *is* small, Mama."

"But of great significance and the Queen told you why."

"Papa had already said much the same," Tilda said. "What I really wanted to ask was whether amongst all those photographs and pictures on the desk there was one of Prince Maximilian."

"I have already told you, Tilda, there are no photographs of him. He does not like being photographed. He will not permit it."

"Why?"

"I am sure that he has a very good reason for his reluctance to be portrayed in the modern fashion for all and sundry to see," Princess Priscilla answered.

"But you don't know the real reason," Tilda persisted.

"I am sure when you meet the Prince he will tell you about it himself," Princess Priscilla replied.

Her tone told her daughter all too clearly that she had her own ideas as to why the Prince had no wish to have his features immortalised by the camera.

It seemed strange to Tilda when everyone else was fascinated by their own likeness.

In every house photographs like the Queen's stood in silver frames on grand pianos, on small tables, on mantelshelves and cluttered writing desks until it was almost impossible to find room for pens and paper.

"I should like at least to have some idea of what he looks like," Tilda persisted.

"I have not seen him since he was a boy," Princess Priscilla said quickly. "But then he was very good-looking and I believe from all reports he is considered extremely handsome."

'If he is,' Tilda thought to herself, 'why should he be so shy and reserved about letting other people look at him?'

There was silence for the moment except for the noise of the railway wheels and the hoot of the engine.

Then Tilda asked,

"Has the Prince seen a photograph of me?"

"Your father enquired when the arrangements for your marriage were first discussed if there was to be an exchange of portraits," her mother replied, "but, when he was told the Prince had never been painted or photographed, he thought it would be embarrassing if he sent him those photographs that were taken of you in January."

"You mean then that like me the Prince is buying a 'pig in a poke'?" Tilda remarked.

Her mother sat up sharply.

"Really Tilda, that is an extremely vulgar and unseemly expression. I cannot think where you have heard it!"

"It is very apposite all the same, Mama, is it not?"

"I am not going to discuss the subject any further," Princess Priscilla said firmly, "If you want to talk about your marriage, Tilda, we can go over the lists of items for your trousseau, which is not yet completed."

"I certainly do *not* wish to do that!" Tilda answered. "I have so many clothes, far too many already. They will last for years and years and years!"

She sighed.

"Can you imagine anything more dismal, Mama, than to think that ten years from now I shall still be trying to wear out my out-dated unfashionable garments?"

Princess Priscilla drew in her lips.

"I cannot think what has happened to you lately, Tilda," she said, "You have become almost revolutionary. I only hope that your Papa will not hear you speak like this. It would annoy him."

"Tell me, Mama." Tilda said, "did you ever when you were young feel like doing something quite different from what people expected you to do?"

Her mother did not reply and she went on,

"Did you ever want to run away for instance when you were told that you had to marry Papa? Did you ever want to stop being yourself and be someone quite different for a change?"

"No, Tilda!" Princess Priscilla said firmly. "I was very grateful and very happy to marry your father. Unlike you I had five sisters and my father and mother continually worried as to where they could find suitable husbands for us all."

Her voice softened as she continued,

"I was twenty-five before I was permitted to make a marriage that did not involve my wearing a crown and I was very lucky indeed that I could become the wife of such a kind and good man as your Papa."

"Not one little thought of rebellion, Mama?" Tilda coaxed.

"Not one!" Princess Priscilla responded firmly, "and you must promise me, Tilda, that you will not allow yourself to even think of such outrageous and wicked ideas."

Tilda did not reply and she went on,

"You have no idea how fortunate you are in being married so young and to a Royal Head of State."

"Do you think that Prince Maximilian wants to marry me?" Tilda asked.

"It is the ambition of every small state in Europe to have one of our Queen's relatives as the wife of their reigning Sovereign. England is a great power in the world, Tilda, as you well know. Every country wants our goodwill, our friendship and, if necessary, our financial aid,"

"Even Germany?" Tilda asked.

"Even Germany!" Princess Priscilla replied, but her tone did not sound quite so positive.

"Prince Bismarck must be a very exceptional man," Tilda went on. "He has formed the Federation of Germany and now Hanover is no longer independent, nor Hesse-Kassel, Bavaria or Brunswick."

"I am glad to see you are so well read," the Princess remarked.

"It is what the Professor has been teaching me," Tilda answered. "You told him to instruct me about the history of Europe and he has been stuffing me with information like a Strasbourg goose!"

"I have the greatest respect for Professor Schiller," her mother replied, "and I intend that he shall travel with you on your journey to Obernia."

"Oh no, Mama! I don't want to spend the whole journey doing lessons!"

"It will be to your advantage, Tilda, and your Papa has asked the Dowager Lady Crewkerne to act as your chaperone and Lady-in-Waiting until you reach Obernia."

"Not Lady Crewkerne!" Tilda cried plaintively. "She is old and dull and disapproves of everything. I have never heard her say a kind word about anybody."

"But she is well-travelled, Tilda. Her husband was at one time our Ambassador in Vienna. She knows all the protocol which is so essential for you to learn so that you do not make any mistakes when you reach the Principality over which you are to reign."

"Lady Crewkerne and Professor Schiller!" Tilda exclaimed. "Well it will certainly be a dull journey. Whatever he is like, I shall jump into Prince Maximilian's arms with joy!"

"I hope you will do that, Tilda, and I am sure you will be very happy," Princess Priscilla said.

She gave a deep sigh.

"I only wish I could accompany you myself, but you know I cannot leave your Papa."

"No, of course not, Mama. At the same time it would be very much more amusing for me than travelling with the two companions you have chosen for me."

"It is very important that you should arrive with a respectable and respected entourage," Princess Priscilla said. "But you do appreciate, Tilda, that a journey such as you are about to embark on is very expensive."

She sighed again.

"We really cannot afford at this moment to send more people with you than is absolutely necessary. As it is, two coaches each with six horses will involve a considerable amount of money."

Although he was extremely rich, the Duke was well known to be parsimonious and close-fisted when it came to spending money outside his estates.

The Princess had experienced some difficulty in extracting from him what she considered enough money for Tilda's trousseau.

"*Two* coaches, Mama?" Tilda asked.

"There will be a coach for the maids and your luggage and apart from your trousseau you will receive many wedding presents which will have to be conveyed somehow to Obernia."

She held up her hand and started to count on her fingers and then continued,

"So that involves – two coaches each with two coachmen and two footmen. That makes eight servants. You will also require four outriders. Even in this enlightened age, travellers can be held up and robbed by bandits on the roads."

"That sounds exciting!" Tilda said, a sudden light in her eyes.

"It is an excitement that I hope you will not experience," her mother replied. "The outriders that your father will send with you are experienced pistol shots and will ensure that you reach your destination in safety."

"I do indeed have a long way to go."

"That is true," the Princess answered, "but you will break your journey by visiting various of our relatives en route, starting in the Netherlands where you will disembark. After a visit to King Ludwig of Bavaria, you will cross the border into Obernia."

"He is the one person I have always wanted to meet," Tilda enthused. "He sounds fascinating!"

Princess Priscilla started to speak and then pressed her lips together, which told Tilda all too clearly that her mother disapproved of King Ludwig II.

Tilda had always been fascinated by hearing about him, his passion for music and the theatre he had built for Wagner.

She had seen portraits of him looking pale and handsome and rather ethereal, as if, she thought, he was a being from another world.

To stay in one of his castles about which there had been so much talk and so much criticism would, Tilda thought, be almost as thrilling as seeing the Palace that would be her home, and more important, her future husband.

"I do hope, Tilda, that you will remember to behave properly!" Princess Priscilla exclaimed. "You heard what the Queen said. You are an Ambassador for England and only by keeping yourself strictly under control will you ever be able to fulfil all our hopes of you."

She looked at her daughter and thought that it would be far more suitable to be planning a school treat for her or a picnic by the river rather than a Royal marriage.

Tilda was lovely in a childlike fragile way that made one think of dolls and flowers, but certainly not of responsibility, of political machinations or of being a married woman.

Suddenly Princess Priscilla felt unexpectedly maternal.

"Oh, Tilda," she said with a throb in her voice, "I *do* want you to be happy."

Tilda smiled.

"Don't worry, Mama," she said. "I am sure that it cannot be as bad or as frightening as it all sounds."

Chapter Two

"It is lovely! It is exactly what a Royal Palace should be!" Tilda cried when they arrived at the *Linderhof.*

She found herself saying it again and again as they went round the fantastic Palace that King Ludwig had built in the green Graswang valley,

"The place owes its name to an ancient lime tree," the King's *aide-de-camp* explained. "Originally on this site there was only a little hunting-box."

"Now it is fantastic!" Tilda exclaimed.

"It has only been finished this year," the *aide-de-camp* went on. "His majesty, inspired by the French buildings of Versailles and the Trianon was determined to create something unique, a jewel amongst the mountains!"

"I have heard," Professor Schiller interposed, "that His Majesty in a letter to Baron von Leonrod said,

'It is essential to create such Paradises, such poetical sanctuaries, where one can forget for a while the dreadful age in which we live'."

"This really is a Paradise!" Tilda said in an awed voice.

It was a compact, very white building designed in an exaggeratedly ornate baroque style and was, she felt, like a Fairy Palace that could only exist in a dream.

The King's huge canopied blue velvet bed, enriched with fantastic gold carvings and surrounded by cupids holding up a crown was such a bed, she thought, as she personally would like to sleep in.

The exquisite yellow, mauve, rose and blue porcelain cabinets to separate the bigger rooms, the Moorish kiosk, the Grotto of Venus and the unbelievable carved gold sleigh in which the King could journey from the *Linderhof* to his castle at *Neuschwanstein*, were all breathtaking.

It was, however, extremely disappointing to find that King Ludwig himself was not at the *Linderhof* to greet them.

She was so looking forward to seeing him and envisaged him a romantic figure such as one could only meet in books.

Because he was known to be elusive and disliked meeting strangers and also because, Tilda thought, she was not of any particular importance, she was not really surprised to find on her arrival that the King was at the lake of Chiemsee.

He was in fact supervising the building of a new Palace, which was to rival the wonders and glories of Versailles.

But with the King or without him, the *Linderhof* was certainly a change from the other places Tilda had stayed at on her journey across Europe.

She had found it tiring and on the whole extremely boring since, except in the Netherlands where the roads were good, the coaches were obliged to go slowly.

The Posting inns where they changed horses were often dirty and unobliging, and the Palaces of her relatives were, to say the least of it, disappointing.

Tilda had not quite known what she had expected, but there was an undoubted air of gloom and perhaps of despondency about them.

This was especially true where the Kings and Grand Dukes had been absorbed into the German Federation and their powers and privileges were being whittled away from them.

Her mother had warned her that she might find this.

"Show all your relatives in those countries more respect than you would accord even to the Queen herself," she said. "They will be very touchy about protocol and want to be reassured as to their status."

Tilda had found that this was exactly the case.

She stood for hours because the King and Queen with whom she was staying would not allow the familiarity of people being seated in their presence.

She found their conversation stilted and to introduce a topic or venture a question was to receive a blank stare of disapproval.

The only person who enjoyed herself was the Dowager Lady Crewkerne, principally because each new place at which they stayed gave her an opportunity to disparage the hospitality they received.

She also acquired more material for her spiteful and uncharitable gossip.

However, most of what she said Tilda could not help feeling was fully justified.

Only when she laughed and sneered at the marriage of King William III of the Netherlands to Princess Emma of Waldeck-Pyrmont did Tilda disagree with her criticisms.

It was true that King William was forty-one years older than his wife, whom he had married the year before. But Tilda realised that the new Queen was happy with her elderly husband and she sensed a happiness in this Palace that she did not find in many others.

Most of her relatives seemed to her to be very old.

Only Frederick I, Grand Duke of Baden was young and good-looking, but it was impossible for her to talk to him alone.

Once again protocol made any conversation seem formal to the point where one yawned almost before one spoke.

'Can I bear a lifetime of this?' Tilda asked herself as they trundled through Hesse-Kassel into Baden, on to Württemberg and across the border into Bavaria.

The *Linderhof* made her spirits rise.

The beauty of the little Palace made her feel that strange surging excitement within her that she had felt when she looked at the Grinling Gibbons carvings in Windsor Castle.

Could anything be more romantic than the Grotto of Venus that King Ludwig had constructed on the slopes of the hillside and where the electric light – the first full-scale installation in Bavaria – could be made to change at will.

On the lake, which could be ruffled by artificial waves, the King kept two swans and a gold cockle-boat in which he could be rowed by a servant.

The garden was also a delight with a fountain whose jet rose to the height of nearly one hundred feet and there were hedges of bleached hornbeam, pyramids of box, cascades, pavilions and a temple.

'Will I find anything like this in Obernia?' Tilda asked herself.

With a little shiver of fear she remembered that however romantic or beautiful the Palace might be she would have to share it with the Prince.

All the time they had been travelling she had been growing more and more apprehensive about the husband who awaited her when she reached her destination.

It was not so much what people said about him but what they said when they thought that she was not listening that concerned her.

She had been sure that there must be something strange about Prince Maximilian when her mother had been so evasive about his reasons for not being photographed.

Now it seemed to her that when his name was mentioned, her relatives put on a special expression that she could not translate into words.

It was disapproval, she was quite sure of that, and she knew too that they were sorry for her.

Once, as she entered a salon, King George of Hanover, who had a large nose and side whiskers that met under his chin, was saying in a booming tone,

"How can that innocent child possibly marry Maximilian? It should not be allowed – "

His words were cut off in mid-sentence when he realised that Tilda was listening. Coughing in a somewhat affected manner he walked away, leaving his wife to face an uncomfortable moment.

After that she listened more attentively. Half-sentences and *sotto voce* comments were disturbing.

"It's criminal, how could they expect that – "

"How can Priscilla allow it? She must know – "

"I just cannot bear to think of that sweet little creature finding – "

What were they hiding from her?

What was wrong?

Neither the Dowager Lady Crewkerne nor Professor Schiller had met His Royal Highness so it was no use questioning them.

Besides Tilda had found that Lady Crewkerne was far too ingrained with diplomatic tact to say anything to her about the Prince that was not extremely flattering.

Tilda faced the fact that there was something definitely wrong.

She tried to think what it could be. Could the Prince be deformed or monstrous in appearance?

But everyone had spoken of him as being good-looking, handsome, in the manner they spoke about King Ludwig.

And there were pictures in the *Linderhof* to prove that here at any rate the adjectives were warranted.

'What can it be?' Tilda asked herself.

As they went further South, she began to wish that she had protested against the marriage from the very start!

Not that it would have done much good if she had!

Both her mother and father had been delighted at the honour that was accorded to her, but perhaps she could have insisted on seeing a picture of the Prince.

Alternatively she could have made a fuss, insisting that the engagement could not be announced unless he came to England and met her.

There were all sorts of excuses and explanations as to why he was unable to do this.

"It is impossible for him to leave his country."

"In his absence it might give Germany an excuse to threaten Obernia's independence."

"It would take up too much time since the wedding is planned to take place in early June."

All the excuses sounded very reasonable and Tilda had accepted them without question.

But now she was suspicious.

What other bride in modern times married a man when she had not the slightest idea of even what he looked like?

Other Kings and Grand Dukes had their features on their coinage, but so far she had not seen any Obernian money.

Linderhof brought to the surface all the dreams that had been hers since she was old enough to think of being married.

It was a perfect background to romance.

It was a Palace where she could imagine herself moving in her beautiful new gowns through the exquisite rooms brilliant with gold, where the very walls seemed to whisper of love.

She stood in the hall of mirrors and saw herself reflected and re-reflected.

Hundreds, no thousands of Lady Victoria Matilda Tetherton-Smythes, and how small and ineffective she looked!

Then she smiled.

She was the right size for the *Linderhof* and in it she could be a Fairy Princess if only there was a Prince to look at her with eyes of love.

Almost like a cold hand placed on her heart she recalled the lecture her mother had given her before she left England.

"You must not expect too much of marriage, Tilda," she had said firmly. "You are making a Royal marriage, a *mariage de convenance*, and therefore you must try to be friends with your husband. You must give him your loyalty and expect his, but you cannot ask for more."

It had seemed to Tilda at the time a cold and austere way to enter into marriage and then she told herself optimistically that everything would be all right.

When she met the Prince, they would fall in love with each other.

She had met very few men, but even her father's friends when they came to the house in Worcestershire would look at her with a little glint in their eyes, which Tilda knew was admiration.

'The Prince will admire me,' Tilda told herself, 'and if he is good looking I shall admire him and then – '

When she went to bed at night, she would tell herself stories of how everything in Obernia would be happy and romantic.

She visualised a smiling cheering people.

She had thought of herself giving out sympathy and understanding to the subjects over whom she would rule and she believed deep down in her heart that the Prince would love her and she would love him.

Now she was frightened.

Frightened by the great gloomy Palaces where she had stayed, most of them crumbling and badly in need of paint and redecoration.

She thought of the Kings and Grand Dukes sitting in heavy silence and carrying on a one-sided conversation with people who could only murmur,

"Yes, Sire," – "Quite so, Sire" and "You are right, Sire," to everything they said.

'I cannot bear it! I cannot listen to that day after day, year after year!' Tilda told herself.

And yet she knew that this was why she had been educated and why she had spent all those hours learning languages!

Why she had read all those heavy history books that never seemed to contain anything but dates and descriptions of battles, births, and deaths.

Why she had studied the maps that had decorated her schoolroom.

Maps of Europe drawn before Napoleon changed the boundaries of almost every country and maps drawn after he had been banished with the countries restored to their original colours.

Now there were maps of Europe after 1871 when the German Federation had been formed.

Now the brown of Germany sprawled everywhere from Russia to France with the acquisitions from the Treaty of Prague in a slightly lighter shade.

'Brown is the right colour for Germany,' Tilda thought. 'It is a dull heavy country. At the same time rather sinister!'

There was something hard and autocratic about the Prussians but, although she had not seen a lot of the Bavarians, she found them different in every way.

They were a smiling people as she imagined that the Obernians would be.

It had been arranged before she left England on the extensive itinerary compiled for her by her father and mother that she should stay at the *Linderhof* for two nights before she crossed the border into Obernia.

As it was only a distance of three miles or so, the Linderhof was really the end of her journey.

After that she would pass into the Principality over which she was to rule and a new chapter in her life would begin.

"King Ludwig of course knows Prince Maximilian well," Princess Priscilla had said, "and he will tell you, Tilda, all the things you want to know before you enter the Capital of your new country."

But King Ludwig, elusive and secretive, was not there and Tilda thought forlornly that she still knew nothing at all about Prince Maximilian.

There was also every likelihood of her making a number of mistakes from the moment she left the *Linderhof.*

On the night of their arrival there had been little time for them to see everything, but on the following day, the *aide-de-camp* had taken Tilda and her companions on an extensive tour of the Palace and gardens.

The place was so small that it did not take long for them to see everything there was to be seen.

Because she was entranced by the exquisite and precise detail that the King had expended on his dream Palace, Tilda had wandered around afterwards by herself.

She looked at the embroidery on the curtains, she stared at the *Sèvres* porcelain peacock and was entranced by the tiny oval rose cabinet.

Here panels on the walls held pictures of the King's ancestors set amongst rose porcelain and the line carving in which the craftsmen of Bavaria excelled.

Only someone with a deep appreciation of beauty, with a soul that could vibrate to what the eye saw and to what the ear heard could have envisaged anything so perfect, Tilda told herself.

She returned to the salon, feeling as if she had walked amongst the clouds, to find general consternation.

"I cannot understand it!" the Dowager Lady Crewkerne was saying. "Are you sure that His Royal Highness understands we are here and waiting?"

"What has happened?" Tilda asked.

There was an uncomfortable silence before Professor Schiller, who was always prepared to be calm and matter of fact, said,

"The preparations, Lady Victoria, for your reception in Obernia are not yet completed."

"Did we arrive here earlier than was expected?" Tilda asked.

"No. It is the date that your father anticipated we would reach Linderhof and the date that His Royal Highness was informed we would be here."

They all, including the *aide-de-camp*, looked so worried that Tilda smiled.

"Well, I am quite prepared to wait indefinitely in such perfect and beautiful surroundings," she said.

First Lady Crewkerne and then the Professor looked at the *aide-de-camp*.

He was not a young man and Tilda had thought from the moment of her arrival that he had a worried rather anxious look about him.

Now it seemed intensified.

"I must explain, Lady Victoria," he said in the voice of a man who is feeling for words, "That this hitch in the proceedings is unfortunate from another point of view."

"What is it?" Tilda asked.

"You cannot stay here, my Lady."

Tilda's eyes widened and, before she could speak, Lady Crewkerne said,

"Are you certain? Would it not be possible to ask His Majesty's permission?"

The *aide-de-camp* shook his head.

"As I have already explained," he replied, "His Majesty will never tolerate any interference with his plans. He expected you for two nights. He made arrangements that you should leave tomorrow. I deeply regret to say this, but that is what you must do."

The Dowager Lady Crewkerne made a sound of exasperation, but she did not speak and, after a moment, Tilda said,

"Then where can we go? I obviously cannot arrive in Obernia until they are ready to receive me."

"I can only suggest," the *aide-de-camp* said uncomfortably, "that you return to Württemberg."

"That is impossible!" Tilda answered. "King Karl was kind enough to have us for three nights, but I heard that he was leaving for Alsace after we had departed."

No one said anything and after a moment she added,

"I would not wish to impose upon him further."

"No, of course not," the Dowager agreed and Tilda knew that Lady Crewkerne, who had not enjoyed herself at Württemberg, would not wish to make another visit there.

"The only alternative" the *aide-de-camp* said reflectively, "is for you to go to Munich."

"To stay in His Majesty's Palace?" Lady Crewkerne enquired.

"I am afraid that too would be impossible," the *aide-de- camp* replied.

Tilda could see that he was very embarrassed at having to refuse them hospitality.

She remembered now many remarks that had been said about King Ludwig's strange behaviour.

People were usually very careful whom they discussed in her presence, but she knew that many of her mother's relatives disapproved of him.

King George of Hanover, always blunt, had commented,

"The fellow's mad! That's what's wrong with him. I always did say so!"

His wife had hushed him into silence and the subject had been changed.

But Tilda had not forgotten.

"Are you seriously suggesting," the Dowager Lady Crewkerne asked, "that we should stay at a hotel?"

"It is a very good one," the *aide-de-camp* answered.

"That is true," the Professor agreed. "I remember it well. A very comfortable and respectable place, which has housed a great number of notabilities."

"The Duke of Forthampton," Lady Crewkerne remarked, "planned this journey for his daughter so that she should not at any time have to sleep the night in a hostelry."

"Well that is where we shall have to stay," Tilda said with practical common sense, "unless we intend to spend the night on a mountain and, as they are still snow-capped, I think it would be very cold!"

She was smiling as she spoke.

Suddenly it all seemed to be an adventure and what was more, although she hardly dared admit it to herself, it was really a relief to think that she had a short reprieve before having to enter Obernia.

The Dowager Lady Crewkerne rose to her feet.

"I cannot think what the world is coming to," she grumbled in icy tones, "when a direct descendant of our gracious Queen must pay to have a roof over her head!"

She swept from the room.

Tilda smiled at the *aide-de- camp*.

"Don't look so worried," she said, "I don't mind. I have longed to see Munich. The Professor has told me much about it."

It had indeed been one of the subjects about which Professor Schiller had become quite human.

He had been a student at the University of Munich and he had, when he was older, taught there for some years.

Whenever he spoke of the town, there was a warmth in his voice and there was an enthusiasm about him that was often sadly lacking in his history and language lessons.

"You must realise, my Lady," the *aide-de-camp* said to Tilda, "that I can only follow the instructions and the orders of His Majesty."

"But, of course, I understand that," Tilda said, "and, as we have been so lucky on our whole journey, we must not complain if there are a few difficulties at the last moment."

She smiled again as she spoke and the *aide-de-camp*, with a little glint in his eye, bowed.

"Your Ladyship is very gracious."

"Now, Professor," Tilda said to her teacher, "I will be able to find out if you exaggerated in all your praise of Munich and whether it is as fine and exciting as you proclaimed."

"You will see, you will see!" the Professor asserted.

Tilda knew that he too was pleased to be going to Munich, delighted to see again the town that meant so much to him when he was young.

The Dowager Lady Crewkerne however was sulky and disagreeable for the rest of the evening.

Tilda did not listen to her croakings.

She was still entranced with the *Linderhof*, determined to imprint every exquisite inch of it permanently on her mind.

'Perhaps one day,' she told herself, 'I shall be able to build something like it.'

It was an intoxicating thought.

That night, when the splendour of the glittering candelabra were reflected in the silver mirrors, she felt as if she was wafted away into a romantic dream where everything she had ever imagined and longed for became true.

Because she could not bear to waste her last hours in the *Linderhof*, Tilda rose early.

Long before Dowager Lady Crewkerne was dressed or the Professor had emerged from his bedroom she slipped downstairs.

She walked through the Staterooms and became so lost in admiration at all she saw that she had to make fulsome apologies for being late for breakfast.

The carriages for some reason best known to Lady Crewkerne and the *aide-de-camp* had not been ordered until eleven o'clock and rather than sit about listening to their apologies, which grew more and more abject, Tilda wandered away into the garden.

It was a warm day for the end of May and the sunshine on the blossom of the trees that surrounded the *Linderhof* Palace made it seem magical.

The whole building gleamed like a pearl and high above stretching up towards the deep blue sky were the snow-capped peaks of the Bavarian mountains.

It would grow much warmer during the day as Tilda well knew, but at night it was still chilly.

She had been glad the night before of a thick feather-filled coverlet for her bed.

Now she had no need for a coat and indeed the sun was already so hot that she was thankful for the shade of her bonnet, which was tied beneath her chin with ribbons that matched her eyes.

She walked up the steps of the garden, which led her behind the house and then she climbed higher still.

The King in planning the formal gardens had left the woods wild and unchanged.

They were in fact a perfect setting for the jewelled wonder of the *Linderhof.*

Yet looking at the silver and white birch trees under which grew wild flowers interspersed with moss, Tilda found herself wondering if anything could be more beautiful than nature itself.

She climbed higher and higher, knowing that when she reached the top there would be a magnificent view of the mountains.

It was tiring and, after a little while, she sat down on a fallen tree-stump.

The trees encircled her.

Then she heard voices a little below her and, looking between the trunks, she saw a man and a woman, hand in hand, climbing up the mountainside.

"It is too far and too exhausting!" the woman was protesting.

She was speaking in German, but Tilda's German was very proficient.

"I want you to see the view," the man with her answered.

He spoke in a deep voice.

Now she could see him through the trees and realised that he was very good looking.

His features were clear-cut and he looked, she thought, like many of the handsome men she had noticed since they had entered Bavaria.

He was wearing the peasant costume that looked strange to her eyes, but at the same time she thought it extremely attractive.

The leather shorts, the green jacket with bone buttons and on his head a jaunty little green felt hat with a brush at the back of it all made up a most becoming outfit.

'Yes, he is more than good-looking, he is handsome!'
Tilda told herself.

Then she looked at his companion.

She was exceedingly pretty.

Her hair was red, but of such a vivid colour that it was doubtful if it was natural.

Her eyes were very large and dark-lashed and her lips very red. They were pouting now as she said,

"It's no use, Rudolph, I cannot go any further."

"But you must having come so far. It's only a step."

"And then another step, and then another – "

"Oh, Mitzi, don't be so faint-hearted," the man called Rudolph begged. "Besides the exercise will do you good."

"I'm tired," she replied. "I don't intend to go any higher and who wants to see a lot of old mountains anyway?"

"You have no soul. That is what is the matter with you."

"But plenty of heart!" Mitzi answered.

"That is true!"

They were standing still as they argued and now he put his arms around her.

"You are looking very pretty this morning," he sighed. "Did I forget to tell you so?"

"You did and I think it extremely remiss of you."

"Well, now I will make up for it," he answered.

He pulled her closely against him as he spoke. Then he kissed her.

Tilda watched them wide-eyed.

She had never seen a man kiss a woman in just that sort of way, so possessively, so passionately.

Rudolph was big and broad-shouldered and Mitzi was, in comparison, small and slight.

He seemed to enfold her, crushing her body against his. Yet there was something very attractive in the way they stood, locked to each other, mouth to mouth.

It was, although Tilda did not realise it, the eternal symbol of love all down the ages.

Finally, when it seemed to her as if the kiss would never end, Rudolph raised his head.

"You excite me you always do excite me, Mitzi! I want you!"

Mitzi gave a little laugh.

"What do you expect me to answer to that?"

"I want you!" he repeated and now there was a deep vibrant note in his voice. "I want you now at this moment and I do not intend to wait!"

"Here? In the woods? You must be crazy!"

"Why is it so crazy? Could anything be more delightful, more natural?"

Again Mitzi laughed, but now he was kissing not her lips but her neck.

He held her closer still, yet somehow she managed to break free.

"If you want me, you'll have to catch me," she laughed provocatively.

Then she was running away from him down the side of the hill, zig-zagging between the trees, running with a swiftness that increased as she went.

"Mitzi! Mitzi!" Rudolph cried.

Then he was running after her heavily and yet with more grace than might have been expected in such a large man.

He also ran quicker than she did, or else she slowed her pace, for halfway down the mountain he caught her.

By craning her head Tilda could still see them.

Once again he had her in his arms and his mouth was on hers.

She waited breathlessly to see what would happen next and then a voice a little way below startled her by saying,

"Your Ladyship, the horses are waiting!"

Reluctantly Tilda turned her head to see the *aide-de-camp*, red in the lace from having climbed up the hill to find her in his ornate gold decorated uniform.

She rose from the tree trunk.

"I am sorry," she said, "I forgot the time."

"We were worried as to where you could be, my Lady," the *aide-de-camp* replied. "Fortunately one of the gardeners saw you taking the steps up the mountains."

"I will come down at once," Tilda assured him.

She took a last glance towards the couple whom she had last seen kissing each other a long way below her, but there was no sign of them. Then she thought she saw a flutter of Mitzi's white skirt.

She could not be certain. It was low on the ground so it might have been a flower.

Anyway she could not explain that she had been eavesdropping.

She climbed down to where the *aide-de-camp* was waiting.

He took her hand and assisted her down the side of the mountain until they reached the stone steps leading up the hill from the garden.

"The woods are very beautiful," Tilda said. "Is anyone allowed in them?"

"This is a fairly isolated part of the country." the *aide-de- camp* replied. "There are no official restrictions on tourists or sightseers, but, of course, His Majesty does not encourage them to come near the Palace."

"No. I can understand that," Tilda remarked.

She wondered who Rudolph and Mitzi might be. Were they a married couple on holiday? she wondered.

She thought they must be. An unmarried girl would not be allowed to go wandering in the woods alone with a man.

And Mitzi seemed very sophisticated.

Tilda was almost certain that neither her lips nor her hair were entirely as nature had intended them.

'I shall never know who they were,' she told herself with a little sigh.

It was like reading halfway through a book and then losing it so that one never knew the end of the story.

In the coach driving towards Munich, Tilda found herself thinking of the strange tone of Rudolph's voice when he had said to Mitzi,

"I want you! *I want you!*"

It had somehow vibrated through her in a way that she could not explain.

She supposed ordinary people, unlike Royalty, spoke in that urgent manner.

It was certainly a contrast to the flat voices and the words that seemed almost to come reluctantly to the lips of those she had conversed with on her journey.

They reached Munich to find the hotel was large, impressive and apparently so comfortable that even the Dowager Lady Crewkerne was mollified.

To Tilda it was an adventure that she had not expected.

In the streets crowded with people, most of the men were wearing Bavarian dress and a large number of women wore red petticoats, black bodices and white embroidered blouses.

There were high houses, which looked impressive and, as they drove through *Marienplatz*, the Professor pointed out proudly the new Town Hall with its steep gables crowned by bell turrets.

Its enamelled copper figures were one of Munich's chief attractions and its *glockenspiel* or *carillon* was, the Professor boasted, the largest in Europe.

"If we have time tomorrow, Lady Victoria," he said to Tilda, "I will take you to the Picture Gallery at the *Alta Pinakothek*. It is built in the Venetian style of the Renaissance and houses the paintings collected by the Wittelbachs since the sixteenth Century."

"I should love that," Tilda answered enthusiastically.

"And there are also Churches that you must not leave Munich without visiting."

"I like Bavarian churches," Tilda said. "I love their gay painted carvings. They are very beautiful!"

"It's a pity we could not stay at the Palace" the Dowager Lady Crewkerne interposed in a sour voice.

"I think it's more fun to stay in an hotel," Tilda insisted. "We have seen so many Palaces, but no hotels."

"Let's hope our stay will not be a long one," the Dowager remarked.

She turned to the Professor.

"Have you notified His Royal Highness where we can be found?"

"I sent a messenger to Obernia this morning before we left Linderhof," the Professor replied. "I feel sure that His Royal Highness will realise our position."

"Let us hope so," Lady Crewkerne muttered.

She spoke in a tone that told Tilda she expected the Prince to be too insensitive to understand what she considered a subtle insult.

'Oh dear!' Tilda thought to herself. 'It seems as if my new life is starting off on the wrong foot!'

Personally she did not mind. This would give her an opportunity to see Munich.

The Professor had been full of its praises about the fine streets, the houses, the museums, the Churches and the University. He spoke about them all as if the City was a paradise for the young and brainy.

And, of course, he had described the beer halls.

He had waxed quite eloquent about how, as a young man, the beer halls had attracted him night after night.

"They were so alive, so amusing," he had told Tilda. "There were artists who sang. Some were from the opera, glad to earn an extra mark or so and there was dancing."

"What sort of dancing?" Tilda asked.

"Country dancing. The men clap their hands and slap the sides of their leather shorts, the audience claps with them and joins in the popular songs."

"It sounds very gay!" Tilda exclaimed.

"It *is* gay," the Professor had agreed, "and there were other performers who would yodel and play the cowbells."

"What does that mean?" Tilda had enquired.

"The leading cow of a herd in Bavaria usually has a bell around her neck so that the cowherd will not lose her. These bells all have a different note"

"I understand! When they shake them one after another it makes a tune."

"Exactly!" the Professor smiled,

"We have bell ringers in England at Christmas in the country," Tilda said, "but their bells have handles."

"These have just a loop through which a string is passed to hang around the cow's neck," the Professor explained. "The men become very proficient at playing tunes of all sorts, even famous ones, on the cowbells."

"Oh, I would like to hear them!" Tilda cried, "and most of all I would like to see the dancing!"

As she spoke, she knew it was something that would never happen, unless, of course, when she was married there was a Command Performance for her and the Prince.

Now she was in Munich she began to think about the beer halls.

Supposing – just supposing she could persuade the Professor to take her to one.

They had dinner in a rather gloomy oak-panelled dining room and as soon as it was over the Dowager Lady Crewkerne rose to her feet.

"I have a headache," she said, "and I intend to retire to bed immediately. I suggest. Lady Victoria, that you do the same."

"I will, ma'am," Tilda agreed. "May I just finish my coffee?"

"Of course," Lady Crewkerne conceded, "and by the way, I forgot to mention it before, but your maid has a bad cold. As I have no wish for you to catch it just before your entrance into Obernia, I told her to go to bed. One of the hotel maids will help you to undress."

"I thought Hannah was looking unwell," Tilda said. "She hates the movement of the coach. It always makes her feel sick. I think she has had a headache ever since she left England."

"Headaches are one thing, a cold is another!" Lady Crewkerne said firmly. "I hope she will be better tomorrow, but she had best keep away from you as much as possible."

She paused and then said,

"Goodnight, Professor."

"Goodnight, my Lady."

Lady Crewkerne went from the dining room and Tilda, having risen as she left, sat down again.

"May I have another cup of coffee?" she asked.

"It will not keep you awake?" the Professor enquired.

"Nothing keeps me awake," Tilda answered, "and the coffee is delicious."

"Bavarian coffee!" the Professor exclaimed, almost in tones of ecstasy. "Even in the villages you can find good coffee with a great spoonful of whipped cream floating on top of it. It's delicious!"

"Do they also have coffee like that in the beer halls?" Tilda asked.

"But naturally," the Professor replied, "and they have long high glasses filled with light sparkling Bavarian beer. It is, my Lady, more delicious than champagne!"

"I would love to try it."

"In the *Hofbrauhaus*," the Professor went on, "which has a long tradition going back to 1589, there is a great vaulted hall where whole barrels are consumed every day."

He saw Tilda was listening with excitement in her eyes and continued,

"Special beers are brewed for celebrated people and for festivals."

Tilda put her arms on the table and bent forward.

"Listen, Professor," she said, "why don't you and I visit a beer hall tonight?"

"Lady Victoria! You must be joking!"

"No, I am serious," Tilda answered. "You have told me so much about the amusing gay beer halls of Munich and I would so love to see one!"

"I would like to show you one," the Professor answered, "but you realise as well as I do that it is impossible!"

"Why is it impossible?" Tilda asked. "Her Ladyship has gone to bed. Hannah is not waiting up for me. Who would know if we crept out, you and I, and went to one?"

"No – no!" the Professor cried. "It is inconceivable!"

"It would be very good for my education," Tilda coaxed. "You see, I think a reigning Princess should know what interests her subjects. It is very difficult to understand these things unless one sees the places they go to, hears the songs they enjoy and watches them dance,"

"I think you are right in your aspirations, my Lady," the Professor responded, "As you know, I have always been very liberal-minded. I think all Monarchs are far too isolated from their subjects."

"Like the Queen at Windsor."

"Exactly!" he agreed. "But it will be up to His Royal Highness to decide how far you can relax the formalities of the old protocol, which keeps Rulers in glass cases."

"His Royal Highness does not seem very interested in me at the moment," Tilda said, "and I should so much like to see a beer hall,"

"I have told you, my Lady, it's quite impossible," the Professor affirmed.

Tilda sighed.

"In which case I shall have to go alone!"

"Lady Victoria!"

There was no doubt of the shocked astonishment in the Professor's voice.

"I will go alone or I will ask one of the waiters to accompany me," Tilda added. "And after it is discovered and I am asked why I did anything so outrageous, I shall tell them that it was all your fault."

"*My* fault?" the Professor groaned.

"Yes. You told me about the beer halls. You described how attractive they are, excited me about them and then refused to escort me to one."

"Lady Victoria, you are teasing me!" the Professor said. "You often play tricks on me and ever since I have been your teacher you have often deliberately tried to provoke me, but this is going too far!"

"I mean what I say," Tilda said. "Either you take me to a beer hall or I go alone."

The Professor passed his hand over his forehead. He was sweating.

"Let's discuss this logically," he begged.

"There is no logic about it," Tilda said. "I mean what I say. I am not going to miss this opportunity."

She gave a little gesture with her hand.

"When else in my life am I likely to be in Munich again with the chance of seeing something real and exciting? Who will it hurt? Who will it harm? Besides, no one will ever know!"

"How can we be sure of that?" the Professor asked.

He was weakening and Tilda knew it.

"I have everything planned," she persisted. "Just listen —"

Chapter Three

Tilda looked at herself in the mirror with satisfaction.

For one terrifying moment she had thought it would be impossible for the chambermaid to find the costume she required.

She had gone upstairs from the dining room leaving an almost incoherent Professor and clutching two gold gulden in her hand.

"You must give me some money, Professor," she had said.

"Money?" he enquired in surprise.

"You know quite well that I have none with me," she answered, "and I shall have to pay the chambermaid to find me a Bavarian costume."

He looked surprised and she explained,

"I do not think it would be wise for us to go to a beer hall looking as we do now. I am sure we should appear conspicuous."

"You are right, Lady Victoria. Of course you are right, but we should not be going to a beer hall at all!"

"Now, Professor, don't let's begin the argument all over again," Tilda admonished him. "You have agreed to take me and all I require at the moment is some money."

He handed her with obvious reluctance two gold gulden and, as she rang the hell in her room, she waited apprehensively.

She had not been sure whether or not the chambermaid who would wait upon her would be young.

There was always the chance that, because the hotel was impressed with the Dowager Lady Crewkerne and herself, it would be one of the older women, who she was afraid would not understand or sympathise with any sort of escapade.

No one in the hotel knew that she was engaged to His Royal Highness, Prince Maximilian of Obernia.

The Duke of Forthampton had been insistent that there should be no publicity and no official announcement until Tilda had safely reached Obernia.

"It might involve you in difficult situations, my dear," he had said to his daughter. "Journalists are very pushing and impertinent and I would not wish you to be subjected to their questions or indeed their cameras."

Tilda had therefore travelled as a tourist, but it was impossible for the inns where they had changed horses, or indeed the hotel where they were staying now, not to be impressed with their coaches, their outriders and in fact the whole entourage.

To her extreme relief after a knock on the door the chambermaid proved to be a young apple-cheeked Bavarian girl who could not have been much older than herself.

"You rang, *gnädige fraulein*?"

"Yes, I rang," Tilda answered. "What is your name?"

The maid curtseyed and replied,

"I am called Gretel, *gnädige fraulein*."

"I need your help, Gretel."

The girl's eyes widened in surprise.

"My help?" she exclaimed.

"Yes," Tilda said, "I am going to trust you with a secret, Gretel."

The girl came a little nearer, obviously intrigued by what Tilda had to say.

"I am going to visit a beer hall with Professor Schiller," Tilda explained. "I want to see one so much, for I have heard how exciting your beer halls are."

"They are indeed," Gretel answered. "Very exciting and great fun, *gnädige fraulein!*"

"Then you can understand why I want to see one – but you must help me."

"How can I do that?"

"I want a Bavarian costume. Do you think you can find one that will fit me?"

The chambermaid looked at Tilda in consternation.

"The *gnädige fraulein* is very small," she said doubtfully.

"You must find me one – please," Tilda pleaded, "and look, I can pay either to buy one or to borrow it for the evening."

She opened her hand as she spoke so that the chambermaid could see the two gold gulden.

"That is too much, *gnädige fraulein!*" she exclaimed.

"That is what I am prepared to pay," Tilda said.

The chambermaid put her fingers up to her forehead.

"Let me think," she murmured. "I am sure I must know someone who has a dress that will fit you."

It seemed to Tilda as if there was a very long wait before she cried,

"I remember! I remember now that Rosa said that she was buying a dress for her little sister, who is to be a bridesmaid at a wedding which is to take place next month."

She paused and added,

"Rosa's sister is only ten, but I feel sure that her clothes will fit you, *gnädige fraulein.*"

"Then please get them for me," Tilda said, "and quickly!"

The maid went from the room and Tilda started to take off the elegant evening gown she had worn at dinner.

She could not help wondering whether the Prince would admire the beautiful dresses that her mother had expended so much money and energy on.

They had all come from a most expensive gownmaker in London and to Tilda, who had always been dressed very simply in the country, they seemed not only lovely but masterpieces of intricate tailoring.

But, she told herself with a smile as she put the gown down on the bed, they would certainly look out of place in a beer hall.

She took off the single row of pearls that she wore around her neck and then looked at the finger of her left hand.

Her mother had not permitted her to wear any jewellery while she was travelling with the exception of her pearls.

"It would be far too dangerous," she said, "for it would undoubtedly attract the attention of thieves and pickpockets."

All the rest of Tilda's jewellery with the presents she had been given by her relations before she left England, and there was quite a lot of it, was therefore in Hannah's care.

She never let it out of her hands and Tilda was convinced that she slept with it, not under her pillow, which would have been too uncomfortable, but beside her in the bed.

Just before Tilda had left England, Princess Priscilla had said,

"You should wear a ring of some sort on your finger, otherwise it will look strange when you arrive at the houses of our relations before Hannah has time to unpack your jewellery."

She had given Tilda a small gold ring in the front of which was entwined two hearts set with minute diamonds.

"How pretty it is, Mama!" Tilda had exclaimed.

"It is only a trinket that your father gave me on our honeymoon," Princess Priscilla replied. "I admired it in a shop window and he bought it for me. I have always treasured it."

"I don't like to take it away from you, Mama."

"I shall be very happy to think of you wearing it," Princess Priscilla replied.

For a moment Tilda now contemplated taking it off, but then she thought that the Professor might think it strange if he noticed it was missing.

She therefore put her pearls in the drawer of the dressing table, but left the ring on her finger.

Gretel returned with the clothes that she had spoken of over her arm.

"Oh, how pretty they are!" Tilda exclaimed.

There was a blouse with intricate red smocking on white muslin, a black bodice that laced down the front, a red skirt, which was worn over three starched white petticoats edged with broderie anglaise and a little apron bordered with lace.

"I am sure they will fit you *gnädige fraulein*," Cretel said, "and there is a wreath to wear in your hair."

She held it up as she spoke and Tilda saw that it was made of artificial flowers with coloured ribbons to fall down at the back.

"Will it be too – elaborate?" she asked hesitatingly, knowing it had been chosen for a bridesmaid's dress.

Gretel shook her head,

"No, *gnädige fraulein*. You will see a large number of girls wearing them in the beer halls. They like to dress up when they go out with their boyfriends."

"My boyfriend is rather old," Tilda smiled thinking of the Professor, "but I would still like to wear the wreath."

The clothes that had been made for a sturdy little Bavarian girl of ten fitted Tilda well.

The skirt was, however, too large around the waist, but Gretel had wisely brought a needle and thread with her and she took it in two inches which made it fit exactly.

"You look very attractive, *gnädige fraulein*," she said.

The skirt ended above the ankle, which made Tilda feel a little embarrassed that she was showing so much white stocking, which was part of the costume.

Then she told herself there was no one to make her feel shy.

The Professor would be far too agitated to look at her and she was quite certain that, amongst all the other Bavarian costumes in the beer hall, hers would pass unnoticed.

At the same time she could not help wondering if a man would think her attractive? Prince Maximilian for instance or the attractive Bavarian she had seen this morning – Rudolph.

She put on her own black slippers and then with the wreath on her fair hair she took a last look at herself in the mirror.

Her eyes were shining with anticipation of what lay ahead, for not only was the costume extremely becoming, but she also looked very young and to herself very gay.

"Thank you, Gretel! *Thank you!*" she cried. "I can never be grateful enough to you. This is really the most exciting night of my life!"

She paused to add,

"You will keep my secret? You will tell no one? Tomorrow you must come to my room very early before I am called to take away the costume."

"I will do that, *gnädige fraulein*," Gretel replied, "but I can collect it when you return. I am on night duty on this floor."

"Then I will ring the bell, but make sure that it is you who will answer it," Tilda insisted.

She gave the chambermaid the two gold gulden to give to Rosa for the loan of the costume and added,

"Tomorrow I will give you two more for yourself because you have been so kind."

"It is too much, much too much, *gnädige fraulein*," Gretel protested.

At the same time Tilda guessed that she was excited at the thought and was doubtless already thinking of the pretty new costume she would be able to buy for herself.

Still feeling a little apprehensive, Tilda walked along the corridor and down the stairs to the first floor.

She had told the Professor not to wait for her in the vestibule, but at the top of the first flight of stairs so that they could take another exit out of the hotel.

She found him there and gave an exclamation of delight.

He too was wearing Bavarian costume.

Even though he was old and inclined to be a little stout, the leather shorts and green jacket looked extremely well on him and only a little strange after the conventional dark suits he wore as a Professor of Languages.

"I brought it with me," the Professor explained a little shamefacedly, "just in case I should go out with some of my Bavarian friends."

"I am very glad you did," Tilda said, "and I feel very proud of my escort. I only hope you don't feel that I might disgrace you."

"You look very charming, Lady Victoria," the Professor said admiringly, "but we ought not to be doing this."

"Come on, Professor, this is not the moment to be fainthearted," Tilda smiled. "And incidentally, I am your niece – Tilda – and you are my 'Uncle Heinrich'. Don't dare to even breathe the name 'Victoria' in case anyone should overhear you."

The Professor groaned, but he did not reply.

Tilda hurried him away down another flight of stairs that led to a side door of the hotel.

They walked into the street.

"Have we far to go?" Tilda asked.

"The *Hofbrauhaus* is not far from here," he replied. "It will not take us more than a few minutes to walk there."

"Then let's walk."

After the heat of the day the air felt pleasantly cool.

It was an excitement in itself to be walking along the streets rather than driving sedately beside Lady Crewkerne in a closed carriage.

The Professor, obviously nervous, walked quickly and Tilda hurried beside him thinking it best not to delay him with conversation.

The streets were well lit with gas globes. They turned down several side roads and then in front of them there were the blaring lights and big doors of the *Hofbrauhaus*.

A large number of people stood in the entrance where there was a desk where they must buy tickets to enter the hall.

The Professor and Tilda had to take their turn.

While they were waiting, Tilda looked about her.

There were a large number of tall brawny young men in Bavarian costume mostly with girls dressed like herself.

There were also several middle-aged and older people obviously accompanying their families and making a night out of it.

The man selling the tickets seemed to take a long time and there were difficulties over change, which made their progress slow.

Then one of the doorkeepers was bowing low and opening the door wider for a couple who were obviously not required to purchase tickets.

Tilda looked at them and felt her heart give a little leap.

It was the couple she had seen in the woods by the *Linderhof.* She would have known them anywhere.

There was no mistaking the handsome face of Rudolph, who was wearing the same Bavarian clothes he had worn that morning.

But Mitzi on the other hand was very resplendent.

Her green evening gown, cut very low and daring, was decorated with bunches of green ostrich feathers and she had a long boa of the same feathers around her shoulders.

There were jewels sparkling in her red hair, which was piled in elaborate curls on top of her head.

Her dark lashes seemed longer and darker than ever and her lips redder.

"Good evening, *mein herr*, good evening, *gnädige fraulein*," the doorkeeper was saying. "Your usual alcove has been kept for you."

"Thank you," Rudolph said in his deep voice, which Tilda remembered.

She saw him give the man a tip as they were shown through a different entrance into the beer hall than the one the ticket-holders were passing through.

It was some minutes before the Professor was able to purchase tickets that admitted them into the big vaulted hall that was quite unlike anything Tilda had ever seen before.

At the far end was a small stage.

At the sides were private alcoves, not unlike small boxes, where the more important and valued customers could have their supper.

The whole of the rest of the hall was filled with small round tables and chairs packed so closely together that it seemed almost impossible to sit down.

But a table was found for the Professor right in the centre of the hall directly in front of the stage and Tilda looked around her with delight.

She could not see Rudolph and Mitzi, but then it was impossible to look into all the alcoves because they were protected by their high sides, some of which were decorated with artificial vines.

"This is *so* exciting!" Tilda enthused to the Professor.

"Are you hungry?" he asked.

"Can you eat here as well as drink here?" Tilda enquired.

"Oh, yes. There are Munich specialities. There are white sausages known as *Weisswurst*, knuckle of pork called *Schweinshaxen* and *Steckerlfisch*, fish on small spits roasted in the oven, which I find particularly delicious."

"Will you order for me what you think I will enjoy?" Tilda asked him.

She noticed the elated note in his voice as he recited the special dishes obtainable in the beer hall.

The Professor gave an order to a waiter in shirtsleeves with a leather waistcoat and a brown apron, who put in front of them cut and salted radishes and some small highly salted pastries.

"These give you a thirst" the Professor said with a smile, "and therefore you drink more beer."

"That is good salesmanship!" Tilda remarked.

She ate one of the pastries and found it delicious.

As she did so, an elderly man who was sitting in front of them and who had been there when they arrived turned his head to say to the Professor,

"Excuse me, *mein herr*, but did you see any trouble outside before you came in just now?"

"Trouble?" the Professor enquired, "what sort of trouble?"

"We heard that the students were rioting. My wife is nervous and wishes to go home, but I have told her there is no reason for her to be alarmed."

"I am sure you are right about that," the Professor said, springing to the defence of his beloved students.

"Sometimes things get rough," the man went on. "Last year one of our friends was injured in a student riot and my wife has not forgotten."

"We certainly saw no trouble in the streets," the Professor answered, "and we walked here."

"There! Do you hear that?" the man gestured at his wife.

"What are they protesting against now?" the Professor asked. "There is always something. It is part of University life!"

"I understand," the man at the next table replied, "that there has been some trouble about the appointment of a new Vice-Chancellor. I understand it is to be Herr Dulbrecht."

"And what is wrong with him?" the Professor enquired, "from the students' point of view?"

"He comes from Obernia," the other man answered. "The students say they wish only to be taught by Bavarians. There is, I believe, a very anti-foreign element in the University at the moment."

"There has always to be some reason for protests and a certain amount of horseplay," the Professor said with a smile. "I do not suppose it will be at all serious."

Reassured by the Professor's words, their neighbour turned to his wife still attempting to placate her.

Tilda felt that they must be up from the country.

The husband at any rate was extremely loth to miss an evening's entertainment and waste the price of their tickets just because of an upsetting rumour.

The place was filling up all the time and just as the food they had ordered appeared a band began to play at the side of the stage.

For the moment Tilda was interested in the sausages, knuckle of pork and the piece of fish that were placed in front of them on the table.

She was also delighted with the huge blue-glazed jug that contained their beer and the long slender glasses they would drink it with.

She tasted the beer and thought it rather sour.

Then she realised that performers were coming onto the stage.

There were six men, all in Bavarian costume, their worn leather shorts showing the vigorous treatment they received night after night from their hard-slapping hands.

They started to dance and the noise from their heavy shoes on the stage, the slapping of their hips and the clapping that went on all round the room was noisy and invigorating.

"It is just as I thought it would be," Tilda said delightedly to the Professor.

She had to repeat herself three times before he could hear her. Then he smiled and nodded his head, clapping his hands together like a boy who has gone back to a reunion at his old school.

The dancers received tumultuous applause and were succeeded by a pretty girl who sang a somewhat soulful ballad about her lover who had been lost in the mountains.

The audience obviously were not in the mood for sentiment and talked loudly throughout her song, waves of smoke from pipes and cigars rising in clouds above the tables and up towards the vaulted roof of the hall.

The next item on the stage made Tilda exclaim delightedly,

"Cowbells!"

They were set on a table and played by a group of four. The result was not only extremely melodious, but undoubtedly very clever.

"Oh, I am so glad to have heard them!" Tilda cried as the act finished.

"I should eat your food. It's getting cold," the Professor suggested.

After the large dinner she had already eaten at the hotel, Tilda was not really hungry, but to please him, because she was sure he wanted her to enjoy what he himself found so delectable, she sampled the white sausages and had some of the fish.

"I am going to order some more beer," the Professor said. "Would you like another glass or would you prefer some white wine?"

"White wine, please," she replied.

She could not bear to disappoint the Professor, but she did not really like the beer. Although it was light, it had a sharp taste and she wondered why men found it so delicious.

The Professor then held up his hand to attract the attention of a waiter.

The band was already beginning to play the opening bars of a new act when suddenly a tremendous noise could be heard outside the hall.

A number of people were shouting and then there was a pistol shot.

Instantly everyone turned their heads.

The noise of voices grew louder and the door burst open with the cry,

"Out! Out! Out!" "Out with foreigners!" "Clear them out of our country!" "Get them out of Munich!"

Those at the back of the Hall sprang to their feet.

Some of the men tried to prevent what was obviously a rabble of students forcing their way into the room.

But the people in front and nearest to the stage moved forward.

The Professor gripped Tilda by the arm.

"We must get out of this," he shouted. "There will be another exit."

The people round them had the same idea.

There was the crash of tables and chairs falling to the floor and the breaking crockery as crowds surged towards the stage like a tidal wave.

There was no question of deciding where one should go and Tilda felt herself carried being along by the people beside her.

The Professor still had hold of her arm and they had to push the people in front of them because they were being pushed themselves from behind.

The noise at the back of the Hall grew louder and louder.

More shots were fired.

Then more voices were screaming,

"Out with the foreigners! Bavaria for the Bavarians! Munich belongs to us!"

Tilda had a brief glimpse of the performers standing on the stage staring at the turmoil that was taking place below them. Then they too turned and ran.

The crowd had carried her and the Professor to the very edge of the stage and she saw that the two double doors on one side of it were open.

Then, as she realised that this was the exit the Professor had spoken about, the lights went out.

As they did so, there went up a great cry, half of anguish and half of amusement.

Now the noise of the invaders was even louder.

"Catch them before they escape! Duck them in the fountains! Give them something to take away from Munich!"

Some of the cries did not sound vindictive or frightening but merely jovial, as if the student or rioter concerned was only playing, but others were swearing viciously in the darkness.

There was a shrill scream and again pistol shots.

The crowd increased its efforts to get away and Tilda found herself swept off her feet so that she was barely touching the ground and simply being carried along by the pressure of the bodies on either side of her.

She reached out for the Professor and finding his hand held on to it tightly.

'Whatever happens,' she thought, 'I must not be separated from him.'

His fingers closed over hers.

Now she felt that he was pulling her with him away from those who seemed almost to suffocate her, so that she was half afraid that she would find it difficult to breathe.

'If I faint in this,' she thought to herself. 'I would be trampled underfoot.'

It was a frightening thought and she held onto the Professor knowing that to lose him would be disastrous.

The passage was almost like a tunnel and then there was a light ahead, as the outer doors must have been flung open.

It was a relief to breathe the cool air after the heat and the smoke of the Beer Hall and quickly Tilda found that she was now outside.

The crowd was running away as quickly as their legs could carry them.

"They are coming round the side of the building," a man shouted.

And a woman screamed,

"They are not far behind! "

Everyone was running and Tilda ran too.

They were in the dark narrow lane with no street lighting or it might have been extinguished.

All she could do was to cling to the Professor's hand.

There were dozens of other people running beside them, having no idea in which direction they were going, but propelled by only one thought – to get away from the Beer Hall and the rioting students.

They ran on until Tilda felt breathless.

Then at the turn of a corner there was a street lamp.

She held on to it feeling that her legs could carry her no further and her body was aching from the pressure of other bodies that had squeezed her so closely in the dark passage of the Beer Hall.

"We have escaped!" she gasped and looked up at the Professor.

For a moment she could not credit it.

She could net believe that she was not dreaming or that her eyes were not deceiving her.

It was not the Professor standing beside her holding her hand, but the man called Rudolph!

If she was surprised, so was he.

He stared at her and then he said,

"I thought you were someone else."

"I-I – thought you were – my – uncle," Tilda said, remembering the plan after a slight hesitation.

As she spoke again there was the sound of shouting and pistol shots.

"Whoever we are we had better get out of here," Rudolph said.

He had dropped Tilda's hand in his surprise at seeing her, but now he picked it up again.

"Come," he said, "we don't want to be caught by those noisy hooligans."

He pulled her away from the street lamp and, keeping in the shadow of the houses, they ran the length of the short lane, turned into another and a few seconds later turned again.

Neither of them looked back, but Tilda was aware that they were not alone. There were people behind them.

Whether they were friend or foe she had no idea.

She only knew that Rudolph was right. It was sensible to get away.

Everything else could be sorted out afterwards and somehow she would find the Professor and Rudolph would find Mitzi, but for the moment it would be madness to go back and look for them.

On and on they ran and then round the corner of what appeared to be a deserted lane they suddenly found themselves in the midst of a crowd of students.

They both stopped dead and instinctively, because she was afraid, Tilda moved closer to Rudolph's side.

Then they realised that these students were not rioting but standing defiantly in the small square and that the Police were present.

Swiftly Rudolph turned and, pulling Tilda by the hand, would have moved back the way they had come, but as they did so, a Policeman saw them.

"Into the centre!" he commanded them sharply.

"We are not with these people, *Herr Oberinspektor,*" Rudolph said.

"Do as you are told! Into the centre!" the Policeman answered curtly.

He had a truncheon in one hand and a pistol in the other and there was nothing they could do but obey him.

They took a few steps forward to join the students, nearly two dozen of them, standing sulkily and yet somehow defiant in the centre of the square.

"What will – happen to – us?" Tilda asked in a frightened whisper.

"It's all right," Rudolph answered, "we shall be able to prove we are not students."

Tilda felt her heart give a frightened leap.

If she gave her real name she was well aware of the scandal that would ensue.

For the future bride of His Royal Highness Prince Maximilian of Obernia to be arrested as a rioting student would be a news story that would undoubtedly be printed in the London newspapers as well as all across Europe.

It would probably mean that the British Embassy would be informed of her behaviour and she could guess what her father and mother would say if they heard about it.

"Please – let's get away from here," she urged Rudolph in a frightened voice.

"I will do my best," he said, "but it's not going to be easy

"What are they waiting for?" Tilda asked.

"I imagine a Police wagon," he answered.

Tilda drew in her breath.

A Police wagon would take them with the students to Police Headquarters.

If she then told them that she was a tourist, they would undoubtedly ask her where she was staying.

Perhaps before they would set her free the hotel would have to vouch for her.

She saw all sorts of complications and difficulties ahead.

Worst of all she could foresee the shocked reaction of her relatives.

She could almost hear the sort of remarks they would make sitting in their cold formal Palaces where they had little or no contact with the outside world.

"Fancy Queen Victoria's Godchild behaving in such a manner!"

"Can you imagine the way that girl must have been brought up to behave in such a fashion?"

"It was obvious to me from the very start that she would not be the right sort of wife for Maximilian! "

It was not him they would be disapproving of now but her.

She could hear their voices, see the expression in their eyes, know that they were looking down their aristocratic noses at her audacity and disreputable conduct.

She found she was holding even tighter to Rudolph's hand.

"Try not to be frightened," he said in a kindly voice.

"We must escape! *We must!*" Tilda insisted.

He made no reply, but drew her slowly and imperceptibly round the students who were standing in the centre of the square.

She saw that he was edging his way towards another road on the opposite side to where they had entered. It was in this direction that the Police kept looking, obviously expecting the wagon at any moment.

'How could I have been so foolish as to have made the Professor take me to the Beer Hall?' Tilda asked herself.

It was all her fault, but to be humble and repentant was not going to get her out of the mess she was now in.

"Here it comes! And about time!" she heard the Policeman say and saw a Police wagon drawn by two horses come down the road towards them.

It was a long, black narrow vehicle with no windows and only two doors at the back through which those who were to be conveyed to the Police Station could enter.

There were two Policemen on the box driving the horses and they entered the square to circle it slowly, turning the horses round to face the road they had just come down.

The Policeman opened the doors and two other Policemen ordered the students to move forward.

"Get in!" they commanded.

Two or three students appeared about to obey.

Then, as if the action galvanised the rest of them into life, they all began to shout.

"Down with oppression! Down with the Police! Down with foreigners! We want Munich to be ours!"

The voices rang out riotously in the darkness and, as the Police began hitting a student who tried to escape, there was a yell from behind, the sound of running feet and voices shouting,

"To the rescue! To the rescue! Students to the rescue!"

Suddenly the whole square was in a turmoil.

There were students carrying banners, others with sticks, and even one or two with knives, fighting with the Police, struggling and screaming.

A Policeman fell over and it appeared as if a dozen students were trampling on him.

One of the men in the front of the wagon seated beside the coachman climbed down to go to his assistance.

The noise was indescribable!

Now Policemen were blowing their whistles and the students, noisier than ever, were shouting them down.

There were several shots.

The Policeman driving the horses bent forward from the front of the wagon to see what was happening.

He was half out of his seat although the reins were still in his hand.

With astonishing speed it was then that Rudolph acted.

He pulled the man from the wagon and, as he sprawled on the ground, Rudolph seized the reins from his hands.

In one movement he picked Tilda up and dropped her into the seat in the front of the wagon.

It seemed to her almost as if she flew through the air and then he was beside her.

He had the whip in his hand and he brought it down on the horses' backs.

They jerked forward, moving at a tremendous pace along the road with the open doors at the back of the wagon swinging behind them.

These made so much noise that it spurred the horses into even quicker efforts to get away from the sound.

There were screams, shouts and yells behind them but Rudolph did not look back.

He was concentrating on keeping the horses in the centre of the road, aware that the wagon swinging behind them could easily turn over.

They were moving so fast that Tilda had to hold onto the sides of her seat to prevent herself from being flung out.

"We have – escaped!" she gasped more to herself than to him.

"For the moment," he replied. "Now not only the students but the Police are after us!"

"Will they – catch us?" Tilda asked apprehensively.

"I hope not," he answered. "I believe that there are few comforts in a Munich prison cell."

He obviously meant to speak soberly, but Tilda could hear the excitement in his voice.

'This is certainly exciting!' she told herself, 'even if it is terrifying!'

They were moving now along roads that mercifully seemed empty and were not, she was sure, in the central part of the City.

The horses were still galloping at a tremendous pace and Rudolph was urging them on.

She realised that he drove well and seemed to know his way. She was sure that he would avoid the main thoroughfares or streets where they were likely to be seen by other Policemen.

They had travelled for only a short while before the houses began to thin out.

Now there were trees and, when they had passed over a bridge, they were in open country.

Rudolph was still urging the horses on until Tilda asked,

"Where are we going?"

"As far away from Munich as possible!"

"But I cannot – I mean – I am staying in – Munich."

"It will not be very healthy for either of us at the moment" he said and now there was no doubt that he was laughing. "Not only are we branded as rioting students but we have also stolen Police property and that, I am quite certain, is a criminal offence."

"But I must go back!" Tilda cried. "They will miss me and they will make – trouble."

"Not half as much trouble as I shall be in if I am caught," Rudolph said.

Tilda was still for a moment and then she asked,

"You have – reasons for not wishing to be – interrogated by the Police?"

"I have indeed!" he replied and now he was no longer laughing.

'I am in the same position,' Tilda told herself.

She wondered as they travelled on in the darkness what he had done.

It could not be anything very bad, she thought. After all, he had seemed happy enough this morning when he had been chasing Mitzi through the woods at the *Linderhof*.

At the same time she could remember hearing stories of interrogations by the Police in Continental countries.

Stories of people shut up in damp dark cells having to prove themselves innocent, unlike in England where one was innocent until proven guilty.

'He is right!' Tilda thought. 'We neither of us want to be caught. Whatever happens, we must avoid the Police!'

But, as they rattled along in the darkness in a stolen Police wagon, it seemed an aspiration unlikely to be fulfilled!

Chapter Four

They drove on and now Rudolph slowed the horses so that they were moving at a more normal pace and the flapping doors did not make so much noise.

The moon, which had been obscured by clouds, came out and everything was touched with the radiance of its silver light.

The road wound, Tilda saw, through a valley with hills rising on either side and silhouetted against the starlit sky were the snow-clad peaks of the mountains.

The wind blowing from the snows was icy and Tilda shivered.

"You are cold!" Rudolph exclaimed, "hold the reins for a moment."

Tilda obeyed him wonderingly. Then she realised that he was taking off his jacket.

"There is no reason for you to give me your coat," she said quickly, "I am quite all right."

"I am much tougher than you are," he answered.

He put his jacket over her shoulders and took the reins back from her hands.

"What is your name?" he asked after a moment.

"Tilda, and thank you for your coat."

"There is no need to thank me, and I am Rudolph."

With difficulty Tilda prevented herself from saying that she knew this already.

"You are a tourist in Bavaria?" he enquired.

"Yes. I am English."

"I thought you must be."

"Why?" Tilda enquired.

"Because only the English could remain cool and calm under such extremely explosive circumstances."

She saw him smile and then he added,

"I feel that really you ought to be crying hysterically on my shoulder."

"I have always been brought up to understand that men dislike scenes, especially when they are concentrating on their horseflesh," Tilda replied.

"You are quite right," Rudolph approved.

"But why are you running away?" Tilda asked, "except, of course, from the Police. You are not a foreigner."

"I am not Bavarian if that is what you mean."

She looked at him in surprise.

"I thought you must be."

"No. I am Obernian."

"Then it is the fault of your country that all this rioting has started."

"How do you know that?" he enquired.

"I was told in the Beer Hall that the students did not like the University's choice of a Vice-Chancellor because he came from Obernia."

"They do not really need an excuse for making a nuisance of themselves."

"The students have always been very powerful" Tilda said. "After all it was due to them that Ludwig I was forced to abdicate."

"The trouble in that instance was a lady called Lola Montez," Rudolph replied, "but I see that you have not neglected your history lessons."

"It is a mistake to visit a country and know nothing about it," Tilda responded demurely.

"That is what I thought when I went to England," Rudolph said, "but I found your history very complicated and sometimes exceedingly dull."

"Do you speak English?" Tilda asked.

"I do," he replied in English, "but not as well as you speak German."

He had a faint accent, but his words were perfectly produced.

"But it is very good!" Tilda exclaimed.

"You flatter me!" he answered.

"As you flattered me when you said I was cool and calm."

"I thought you behaved extremely bravely in very difficult circumstances."

"Thank you," Tilda said, "but what are we going to do now?"

"Quite frankly I don't know," Rudolph replied.

"We shall have to do something."

"Well, one thing is quite obvious and that is that we cannot return to Munich."

"But I must!" Tilda exclaimed, "You don't seem to understand – "

"I *do* understand," Rudolph contradicted her, "but you must be sensible. To go back at this moment would be either to encounter the students, who are attempting to purge the City of foreigners, or even worse, to explain to the Police why we have 'borrowed' their wagon."

Tilda gave a little sigh.

"Then what do you suggest we do?"

"I think we must find an inn and stay there for the night. Tomorrow things may have quietened down and you at any rate will be able to go back to Munich."

"If you drive very much further away from the City," Tilda said practically, "It will either be on my feet or riding one of these horses!"

He laughed.

"It is certainly a problem!"

Tilda was looking ahead and now in the distance she saw some lights.

She thought they must come from a cottage but then realised that the lights were actually on the road.

"There are lights ahead of us," she said to Rudolph.

He drew in his horses and pulled them to a standstill.

"I might have had the sense to remember," he said in a low voice, "that when there is rioting in the City the Police barricade the roads."

"You mean – we cannot go any – further?"

"I mean that to do so would be to ask for handcuffs."

He stared ahead at the lights and then looked at the road where they had come to a standstill.

It was narrow with trees growing right down on to the very edge of it.

He pulled the horses to the right and Tilda realised that he was trying to turn them.

"It's going to be very difficult to turn round here," she said.

"I know that," he answered. "Look back and see if there is anyone coming."

It was difficult to do so, but by half-hanging out of the front of the wagon Tilda could still see the lights in the distance.

She suddenly realised that, if she had seen the Police, they would have seen them. There were two lights on the front of the wagon and those watching would undoubtedly have noticed them approaching.

"I think it's all right," she said doubtfully.

But, as Rudolph struggled to back the horses and bring them forward again, she gave a little cry.

"There is someone coming! Two men on horses!"

She heard Rudolph swear beneath his breath and then with a great deal of difficulty, bumping over the edges of the road, he forced the wagon round.

He brought the whip down on the horses' backs, but now they were tired and, although they jerked forward, the wild speed with which they had left Munich was lacking.

"Try to look round and tell me what you can see," Rudolph asked in a voice of authority.

Hanging on tightly to the side of the wagon for fear she might fall into the road, Tilda did as he asked.

"They are still some distance away," she said, "but coming nearer."

"There is only one thing we can do," Rudolph said, "I am going to slow down the horses and I want you to jump out."

"I am not going to leave you," Tilda said in sudden fear, "I cannot be left here – alone."

"I will come with you. As soon as you reach the ground, scramble up the side of the hill keeping in the shadow of the trees."

"Promise – you will – come too," she pleaded in a breathless little voice.

"I promise." he answered. "Do as I tell you. It is our only chance."

He pulled in the horses as he spoke and, when they were moving more slowly, he said to Tilda,

"Now – *jump*!"

She did as he ordered and found herself sprawling on the grass at the roadside.

"*Run!*" he shouted.

Picking herself up, she started to run up the side of the hill, moving between the tree trunks.

She thought that Rudolph had broken his promise as the wagon pulled away and she was aware that he was whipping the horses into greater speed.

Then, as she stood apprehensively beside a tree trunk, she heard him scrambling up behind her.

He reached her side and took her hand in his.

"Come!" he said. "The sooner we get out of here the better!"

'Do you think they will have seen us?' she wanted to ask, but he was moving so quickly it was impossible for her to speak.

He dragged her up the side of the hill and they had gone some distance when Tilda heard the sound of horses' hoofs and a man's voice.

"They must have seen us," Rudolph said. "I hoped that they would follow the wagon."

He started to climb higher.

Now there were rocks and stones on their path, which hurt Tilda's feet. Once she half-fell and in saving herself grazed the palm of her hand on a rock.

It was then that she heard a voice behind them shout,
"Stop! Stop or we shoot!"

Rudolph heard too and climbed ever quicker.

The trees were planted closer together and the shadows seemed dark and impregnable.

'They cannot see us,' Tilda told herself consolingly. 'I am sure they cannot see us.'

"Stop!" the Policeman called again.

Now there was a pistol shot, which seemed to echo eerily through the woods and round the mountains coming back to them with a booming sound.

"Come on!" Rudolph said. "We will be out of their range in a moment."

Tilda was finding it increasingly difficult to keep up with him.

His legs were so much longer than hers and besides the stones slipped beneath her feet so that time and time again she only just saved herself from falling.

It was then that two pistol shots rang out one after another and Rudolph gave a hoarse cry.

"They have hit you?" Tilda asked anxiously.

"Yes, curse it!" he answered, "In the leg."

He hobbled a few more steps and then leant against the trunk of a tree, his face towards the mountain. Tilda knew that the Policemen below would now not be able to see him.

She crouched down beside him on the ground looking up apprehensively.

"Are you all right?" she asked.

"Are they still behind us?" he enquired.

It was impossible to see what was happening through the trunks and the boughs of the trees.

Listening, Tilda could no longer hear the sound of horses nor of pursuers climbing up behind them.

In fact there was silence.

Then far away below she heard the clatter of hoofs on the road.

As she listened, she had held her breath and now it escaped in a deep sigh of relief.

"They have gone," she whispered.

Rudolph did not answer and after a moment she said in a frightened voice,

"Are you – all right? What shall we – do now?"

"I think I am right in believing that there is a village not far from here," Rudolph replied. "We had better try and reach it."

Tilda was about to protest that any encounter with people might prove dangerous.

Then she realised that not only was he wounded but there was a cold icy wind blowing down from the mountaintops.

For the moment she was warm not only from climbing up the hillside but also because she was wearing Rudolph's coat.

He was only in his shirtsleeves and, because it was a white shirt, it had been a target for the Police.

"You are right," she said. "We must find a village. Rest your arm on my shoulders."

She thought that he was about to refuse and then he did as she suggested and they turned to walk not any further upwards but in a straight line along the side of the hill.

After a few moments she realised that Rudolph was dragging his leg.

Then he started to hop.

"You cannot go very far like that," she said.

"What is there ahead?" he asked.

"I can see nothing at the moment," Tilda answered.

They went on a little further and she realised now that it was agony for Rudolph to keep going.

She could see in the moonlight his mouth set in a firm line and she could feel his arm on her shoulders growing heavier and heavier.

Unexpectedly the trees began to thin a little and a moment later Tilda gave a cry.

"There is a house!" she said. "A house right in front of us!"

"I hope I can make it there." Rudolph said, "If not, you will have to fetch someone to help me."

"I am sure – you can manage it."

Again he was hopping on one leg and dragging the other behind him.

Although the house was not far away, it seemed to her to take an immeasurable amount of time before they finally reached it.

It was very small and, unlike most Bavarian houses, only a bungalow.

In the moonlight she could see it was painted white with a black roof. There were two window boxes on either side of the front door filled with flowers.

Rudolph supported himself against the side of the house.

"Knock!" he urged her.

There appeared to be no knocker and Tilda rapped sharply with her knuckles on the wooden door.

There was no answer and she looked around the side to find a window.

She peered through it and saw as the curtains were not drawn that she was looking into a small kitchen.

She went back to Rudolph.

"I don't think there is anyone at home."

She knocked again, then tried to rattle the handle in case that would attract attention.

To her surprise the door opened.

She walked in and found, as she had seen through the window, a small kitchen with a sink, a table and two chairs, a stove in one corner and a primitive range where the owner obviously cooked.

'Perhaps they have gone to bed,' Tilda thought to herself.

There was only one door leading out of the kitchen.

She knocked, but there was no reply and she opened it.

Again the windows were uncurtained and in the moonlight she could see a large bed occupying almost the whole room.

Whoever the owner might be, he was away from home.

It was important now, Tilda knew, to see to Rudolph's wound.

She went back to find him still leaning against the wall, but his eyes were closed and she could see even by the moonlight that there was an unnatural pallor to his skin.

"Come inside," she said, "there is no one here. I can look at your leg."

As if it was too much effort to argue, Rudolph put his arm across her shoulders and let her lead him into the bedroom.

She helped him down onto the bed and she had the feeling that once he stopped walking it would be impossible for him to go on again.

As he took his arm from her shoulders, she saw that there was a candle standing by the bed and beside it a box of matches.

She picked them both up in her hand and crossing the room pulled the curtains.

There was always the chance that the Police might still be in the vicinity and to see a light flare out in the darkness would make them suspicious.

She went into the kitchen and pulled the curtains there too and then she closed the front door.

Putting the candle down on the table, she lit it and as she did so she saw there were two more on a shelf.

She lit these from the first candle and took two back into the bedroom.

Rudolph was sitting forward with his elbows on his knees and his head in his hands.

Tilda set the candle down on the floor beside him and with difficulty stifled the exclamation of horror that rose to her lips.

He had pulled down his stocking and there was blood pouring from the calf of his leg. Blood had also seeped onto the floor in a crimson pool.

With an effort she forced herself to remember what she had learnt about wounds.

It was her mother who had insisted that Tilda should have lessons in bandaging before she left England.

"You are travelling right across Europe," she had said. "There are certain to be minor accidents on the way and, if you do not know how to treat them, it will be impossible for you to tell other people what to do."

She did not add, although Tilda knew she was thinking of it, that there had been recently many anarchist attempts on reigning Monarchs.

An assailant had years ago fired a pistol at Queen Victoria. The Prince Consort had behaved with conspicuous bravery and shielded her body with his.

The year before there had been an attempt on the life of William I of Germany.

There were always incidents of some sort or another and Tilda found herself hoping that, if she and Prince Maximilian were attacked either by men with pistols or by bombs, she would behave bravely and he would not be ashamed of her.

She thought now that her training would be put to good use.

The first thing obviously must be to remove the woollen stocking that Rudolph was wearing and which was already soaked with his blood.

'I must have something to put it in once I have taken it off,' Tilda thought sensibly and went back to the kitchen.

She found a basin and then looked around for some towels.

'Perhaps I can tear one into strips and make a bandage,' she told herself.

She wished now that she had paid more attention to the lessons in bandaging, which she had found boring and at times, when the instructor was explaining the arrangement of the arteries in the body, complicated.

She looked around the small kitchen.

There were some cloths by the sink that had obviously been used for drying the plates and dishes, but she knew that these would be unhygienic.

Then she saw that there was a tall white cupboard in one corner of the room. Perhaps there would be clean towels of some sort there.

She opened it and found herself looking at a shelf on which there were quite a number of bandages, cotton wool and towels of different sizes and materials.

'This is lucky!' she thought.

She wondered if the owner of the house was a nurse or a guide who escorted those who climbed the mountains.

Tilda had heard that the guides always carried bandages as well as brandy.

Taking all she would need from the shelf, she went back to Rudolph.

There seemed to be more blood than ever on the floor.

"I have to try to stop your leg from bleeding," she said.

"I am sorry to be such a nuisance," he replied rather hoarsely.

She undid the heavy brogue shoes he wore and drew the first one from his uninjured leg.

She thought as she did so that as soon as she had bandaged his wound he must lie down.

It was hard to think coherently, but somehow she managed to act slowly so as not to hurt him.

She took off the other shoe, drew the blood-soaked stocking from his leg and put it in the basin.

She vaguely thought that she ought to wash the wound, but there was no reason why it should be dirty and it had been bleeding so freely that any dirt must have washed away.

Now she could see that the bullet had caught him sideways and had seared its way across his calf.

She was almost sure that it was not lodged inside but had merely cut its way along the flesh. But she was not experienced enough to be completely certain.

She did know, however, that Rudolph would be feeling weak not only from the pain but also from the loss of blood.

She made a pad as she had been taught to do and with some difficulty bandaged it into place.

She knotted the bandage in front hoping that the pad would prevent any more blood from pouring down his leg, knowing that if the leg should bleed any more it would leave a terrible mess on the bed.

She looked round and saw on the floor beyond where Rudolph had left a pool of blood that there was a rough mat, such as the peasants made for themselves, of coarse red and blue wool.

Tilda picked it up and laid it on the bed where his feet would rest.

As was to be expected in Bavaria, there were no blankets, but there was a feather eiderdown, a *düchent*, as it was called in German, which was both warm and light.

Tilda pulled it back.

"You must lie down," she said to Rudolph. "You will be far more comfortable. Can you lift your leg onto the bed or would you like me to help you?"

"I will manage," he answered her.

But in the end she had to help him and he lay back with a little sigh against the pillows.

She saw then that for the moment at any rate no blood had seeped through the pad and the linen she had bandaged him with.

With a towel she mopped up the blood on the floor as best she could and carried the basin into the kitchen.

It looked unpleasantly gory and she thought with a smile that it was a good thing she was not squeamish like many of her contemporaries who reputedly fainted at the sight of blood.

As she put the basin in the sink, she remembered that the only way to remove bloodstains was with cold water.

She filled the basin from a jug that she found standing on the floor. It looked frighteningly red and she turned away from it with a little grimace of disgust.

Then she went to the shelf that she had taken the bandages from.

She hoped to find a bottle of brandy so that she could give Rudolph some of it to drink.

She was well aware that he was in considerable pain.

All the time she had been bandaging him and helping him to lie down on the bed, he had been gritting his teeth and she knew that it was to prevent himself from swearing at the pain he was suffering.

There was no brandy, but there were a few medicine bottles and by the light of the candle Tilda inspected them carefully.

One made her eyes light up.

She knew the German word for laudanum and this was what the bottle contained.

'I will give him some,' she thought. 'It will make him sleep and at least he will not be in such agony.'

She had had a Governess once who had always taken laudanum to make her sleep when she had a headache.

It was the universal panacea for most feminine ills and, while medically it was doubtless out of date, it was still, Tilda knew, a very effective form of escape from pain.

She found a spoon and carried the bottle into the bedroom.

Rudolph was lying back with closed eyes.

"I have found some laudanum," Tilda said. "I suggest you take some. It will prevent you from feeling the pain and, as it will also make you sleep, you will undoubtedly feel better in the morning."

"Have you locked the door?" he asked.

"No," Tilda answered.

"Then go and lock it," he said. "I want to make sure you will be safe."

Tilda put the bottle and spoon beside him and did as she was told.

She could not find a key, but there was a wooden bolt, which she pressed home.

'I must get up early,' she told herself, 'to open it again. If the householder comes back and cannot get into his own home, he will think it very strange to say the least of it.'

But this was not the moment to worry about the morning.

She went back to the bedroom.

"I have bolted the door," she said to Rudolph. "Now take some laudanum. It really will help you."

She tried to remember how many drops Miss Grover, for that was her Governess's name, had taken.

But all she could recall was that they had made continual trips into the village in a pony cart to replenish Miss Grover's supplies of what she called 'my headache drops'.

Rudolph raised himself on his elbow, watching Tilda half- fill the spoon and put it into his mouth.

"You had better give me more than that," he said.

"I am not certain what the correct dose should be," Tilda told him.

"Give me the bottle."

He took a swig, wrinkled his nose at the unpleasant taste of it and then took another.

"I am sure that is more than enough," Tilda said in alarm. "I don't want to be left tomorrow with all the explaining to do."

"I will do the talking," he assured her.

He put the bottle into her hand and flopped back onto the pillows as if it had been a tremendous effort for him to raise his head.

Tilda looked at his leg.

There was still no sign of blood through the bandages and now she pulled the *düchent* over him.

"Try to sleep," she said softly.

"Thank you," he said a little drowsily. "Thank you for all you have done for me."

She had the feeling that he spoke with difficulty and she went into the kitchen.

She put back the bandages she had not used, averting her eyes from the bowl that appeared to be full of blood and returned to the bedroom.

Rudolph was already asleep.

He was breathing heavily and Tilda had a sudden moment of panic in case he had taken a fatal overdose of laudanum.

Then she told herself that an overdose would not kill him, but only make him sleep a little longer than was necessary.

She was suddenly conscious of feeling very tired herself.

It had been a long day.

The exhausting scramble up the side of the hill, the fear she had experienced when they had been pursued by the Police and the shock of Rudolph being shot made a sudden wave of exhaustion sweep over her.

She looked around the room.

There was one hard chair, the same sort as she had found in the kitchen.

She had thought vaguely that there might be a comfortable armchair where she could sleep, but there was nowhere except the bed.

It was then she realised that it had grown even colder.

They were high up on the mountainside and she could hear the wind outside howling eerily.

She was still wearing Rudolph's coat, but she could feel herself shiver.

Her legs in their white stockings seemed almost frozen.

She went into the kitchen.

There had been a fire in the range earlier in the day, but now it was out and so was the stove that stood in the corner of the room.

A gust of wind shook the windows.

She blew out the candle before she went back into the bedroom.

She sat down on the other side of the bed from where Rudolph was sleeping.

'Mama would be very shocked!' she told herself.

But Princess Priscilla was not there and Tilda thought with practical common sense that if she had pneumonia in the morning she would only be an embarrassment to everybody including Rudolph.

She sat down determinedly on the edge of the bed and, lifting the feather *düchent*, slipped her legs under it.

It was warm and comfortable.

She slipped a little lower and, turning her back towards Rudolph, she pulled it up high over her shoulders.

*

Tilda opened her eyes, wondering where she could be.

There was sunshine coming through the sides of the curtain that covered the windows.

Then she realised that she was fully dressed and wearing a tweed jacket.

She remembered their wild escape from Munich in the Police wagon, the moment of terror when they had run up the side of the mountain pursued by Policemen on horseback, the blood that had seeped from Rudolph's leg onto the floor!

It all came back to her and as it did so she heard the handle of the door turning and someone pushing against it.

She knew then what was happening.

The owner had returned to find his own door bolted against him.

She jumped out of bed, ran in stockinged feet into the kitchen and across to the door.

Pulling back the bolt, she found outside an elderly woman who looked at her in astonishment.

"Who are you – and what are you doing here?" she asked.

She was a large woman with greying hair, but with a clear pink and white skin and dark blue eyes.

"I must explain, *gnädige frau*," Tilda said quickly. "We sheltered here last night."

"So I perceive! And who is 'we'?" the woman asked, walking into the kitchen and putting a basket she carried on her arm down on the table.

She glanced at Tilda's left hand as she spoke and almost automatically an explanation came to Tilda's lips.

"My – my husband," she said, "we were in – trouble – terrible trouble from the – students."

"I heard they were rioting," the elderly woman said. "Tiresome young men! They ought to be stopped! I have said so over and over again. They ought to be stopped!"

"The Police tried to – arrest us because they thought we were students," Tilda went on breathlessly, "and my – my husband was shot in the leg."

"Shot?" the woman ejaculated. "Where is he?"

She walked into the bedroom.

Rudolph was still asleep, still breathing deeply.

She looked down at him and then her eyes caught sight of the bottle of laudanum that Tilda had left on the table beside the bed.

"So that is what you have given him?" she said.

"I am afraid he took too much," Tilda explained, "but he was in such pain. I bandaged his leg. I hope I did right."

The woman pulled back the eiderdown and Tilda saw that now the bandages were bloodstained,

"I did the best I – could," Tilda said apologetically. "I found the bandages on your – shelf."

"You must have been glad to see them," the elderly woman remarked.

Now she looked at Tilda, taking in her small frightened face framed with fair hair, the green tweed Bavarian jacket over her peasant's dress.

Quite suddenly she smiled.

"You seem very young to be in trouble with the Police and to be bandaging a wounded man."

"I hoped there would be – someone in the house," Tilda said, "but the door was open and anyway I could not have made him walk any further."

"I think you did very well to get him as far as you did," the woman remarked. "Now let me introduce myself. I am Frau Sturdel and I am a midwife."

"So that is why you had bandages and towels!" Tilda cried.

"Exactly!" Frau Sturdel answered. "I have been attending a confinement. Which was why I was not at home."

She went back into the kitchen and Tilda followed her.

"I am very sorry if we have made such a mess of your house," she said, "but we can pay for any damage we have done."

She spoke confidently.

Although she had no money herself, she had felt a fat purse in the pocket of Rudolph's coat and, because of the respect with which he had been welcomed at the Beer Hall, she felt he must be comparatively well to do.

"I don't suppose you have done any harm," Frau Sturdel said, "and now tell me your name."

The question took Tilda by surprise.

"I am Tilda," she said, "and he – " with a little gesture of her hand, " – is Rudolph."

She saw that Frau Sturdel was still waiting and added the first German name that came into her head.

"Weber," she said. "Our name is – Weber."

"And now, Frau Weber," the midwife said, "I will see to your husband's leg. While I do so, I suggest if you don't want anyone to know you are here that you clean the doorstep!"

"The doorstep?" Tilda questioned.

"There is a large pool of blood, which would certainly attract the attention of anyone who should call to see me," Frau Sturdel explained.

"We must not be seen!" Tilda cried frantically. "No one must know we are here. We will go away as soon as we can."

"From what I have heard in the village this morning," Frau Sturdel answered, "It would not be safe for you to return to Munich at the moment. They are still trying to drive out all foreigners!"

She laughed.

"It's the students' regular protest from time to time. Nobody pays much attention to them. But I can see you are not Bavarian."

"I am English," Tilda said, "and my husband is Obernian."

"Then you are Obernian too," Frau Sturdel said, "but that will not help you where the students are concerned. They hate Obernians. In fact they hate everybody except themselves!"

While she had been talking, Frau Sturdel was taking off her coat and replacing it with an apron.

Now she was taking fresh bandages from the shelf in her cupboard.

"Come along, Frau Weber," she said briskly. "That doorstep needs cleaning. A neighbour might drop in at any moment."

Tilda looked around her.

She had never scrubbed a step or anything else.

'I will need a bucket, a scrubbing brush and presumably some soap,' she told herself.

As if she guessed what she was thinking, Frau Sturdel said,

"Under the sink you'll find all you need and a bit of matting to kneel on. I expect you find that scrubbing is hard on the knees."

"Yes – of – course," Tilda stammered.

She picked up the bucket and said hesitatingly,

"Where – do I find – the water?"

"There is a pump in the garden. It's a bit stiff, but I'm sure you'll manage it. The water comes from the hills. Icy

~92~

cold it is at this time of the year. That reminds me, I'd better light the stove."

Uncertain of what she should do, Tilda went into the garden, which contained a few rows of vegetables and some chickens in a wire enclosure,

The pump handle was certainly stiff and the water was slow to emerge even when she had it working.

Finally she half-filled her bucket, knowing that if it was full she would have difficulty in carrying it.

Then she went down on her knees and for the first time in her life scrubbed a doorstep.

She was quite pleased with the result when she had finished.

Then she remembered that Rudolph's leg had been bleeding as they struggled from the wood.

There was therefore every likelihood that he had left a trail of blood on the path to the house that would be noticeable to an astute Policeman.

She retraced their steps of the night before and soon found little patches of dried blood on the gravel and the moss.

She obliterated them and finally carried her bucket and brush back into the kitchen.

"Have you finished?" Frau Sturdel called out from the bedroom.

"Yes, you cannot see the stain now," Tilda replied proudly.

"Then bring in some wood for the stove," Frau Sturdel called. "You'll find a pile of it behind the house."

It took Tilda some time to bring in what she thought would be sufficient to keep the stove going through the day.

When she had completed that task, Frau Sturdel came from the bedroom to throw Rudolph's bloodstained bandages into the sink.

"Put those to soak, dear" she said. "Your husband will be more comfortable now."

"Is he awake?" Tilda asked.

"He's sleeping like the dead!" Frau Sturdel said with a laugh. "Heaven knows how much laudanum you gave him!"

"It will not – hurt him?" Tilda enquired anxiously.

"No, it won't hurt a strong young man like him!" Frau Sturdel answered. "But his leg will be painful for a day or so. A wound on that part of the calf always seems to hurt more than anywhere else."

"There is not a bullet lodged in it?" Tilda asked.

"If there was, I would have found it," Frau Sturdel said. "You can trust me to look after your man for you. I am very experienced, as anyone in these parts will tell you."

"I am not questioning your ability," Tilda replied. "You have been so kind and I am very grateful. It is just that I am so worried about him."

"I suspect you have not been married for very long," Frau Sturdel said archly.

"No," Tilda answered.

"Ah, well, he'll soon be playing the lover again. You need not worry about that! What's more important now is for you and me to have something to eat. Did you look to see if the hens had laid any eggs?"

"No, I did not think of it," Tilda answered. "Shall I go out now?"

"I'll do it," Frau Sturdel said. "You get the saucepan ready."

When it came to cookery, Tilda was more at home. She had always wanted to cook and as a child had a special little house in the garden where she was allowed to make cakes for her dolls.

As she grew older, she had worried their cook until she could try her hand at baking.

Also with her parents she had gone on picnics when she had been allowed to cook on an open fire the trout that her father caught in the lake near their home.

Frau Sturdel, however, did not suggest that Tilda should cook the eggs for their breakfast.

She managed competently and they sat down at the small kitchen table.

Frau Sturdel had bought fresh bread from the village and a block of golden butter. There were also strong-tasting garlic sausages, which Tilda privately thought rather unpleasant.

"When do you think my husband will wake?" she asked, as they finished their meal and carried the dirty plates to the sink.

"It depends how much laudanum you gave him," Frau Sturdel answered. "Judging by the way he is sleeping, I shouldn't be surprised if he doesn't open his eyes until tomorrow morning."

"Oh, dear!" Tilda exclaimed.

"Don't worry about him," Frau Sturdel said. "A good sleep hurts no one."

She did not realise that Tilda was worried because a whole day must pass before she could return to Munich.

She could imagine the consternation of those in the hotel!

At this moment they would be worrying about her and she felt sorry for the Professor who would have to explain his part in her disappearance.

At the same time if the students were still rioting about the streets, it was obvious that she would not be able yet to rejoin Lady Crewkerne and she hoped that the Dowager and the Professor would have the good sense to keep her absence to themselves.

It would be unfortunate if Prince Maximilian should choose this moment to invite them into his country.

'It is all his fault in the first place,' Tilda told herself. 'If we had been allowed to arrive on the date planned by Papa, none of this would have happened!'

And yet she found herself thinking that it was all an adventure and an excitement she would not have wanted to miss.

It had been thrilling in a frightening sort of way to escape from the Police in the wagon and to run with Rudolph up the side of the hill.

As she thought of it she wondered if he had remembered that only that morning he had been chasing Mitzi down a mountain.

She recalled the strange note in his voice when he had called out,

"I want you! *I want you!*"

What did he want? What did he mean when he said those words?

She was so deep in her thoughts that she felt herself start when Frau Sturdel said,

"He will be more comfortable like that."

"Like what?" Tilda asked.

"I have just been telling you," Frau Sturdel replied. "I put him into one of my husband's nightshirts."

She gave a sigh.

"It may seem strange my still keeping them after being widowed for five years, but then I always was sentimental."

She paused and then went on,

"It will give you a chance to wash your husband's shirt, but if you hang it on the line, keep it well at the back of the house. People might think it strange for me to have a man's clothing flapping in the wind!"

She laughed at her own joke and then she continued,

"When I come back tonight, I'll bring you a nightgown. The woman I am attending can quite easily spare one. Anyway I'll say I want to mend it for her."

"It is so very kind of you," Tilda said, "but – "

"She's more your size than I am," Frau Sturdel went on, "and I expect you want to look pretty for your husband as you've not been married for very long."

"Thank you," Tilda said.

There really seemed to be nothing else she could say.

"I'll not forget," Frau Sturdel said, "but now I must be going. You'll find some food in the larder, if your husband is running a fever, which he might do after a wound like that, give him something light to eat such as eggs. You will find both eggs and sausages."

"Thank you very much," Tilda said. "You will be back this evening?"

"I shall be back at six o'clock to feed the chickens."

"And what about the night," Tilda asked. "We must not turn you out of your bed."

"You are not doing that, my dear," Frau Sturdel replied. "I have to be with my patient. The baby is due at any moment, but you know what babies are! It may arrive this afternoon or wait a week! Anyhow I must be there!"

She lowered her voice, as if someone was listening, to add,

"She's not a strong girl. She's not Bavarian, but comes from Alsace. They've not the stamina we have! I only hope she pulls through all right."

She picked up her shopping basket.

"Well, all I can say is it won't be my fault if she doesn't. Take care of yourself. You'd better bolt the door after I have gone."

"I will do that," Tilda said.

She watched Frau Sturdel going heavily down the hill by a path that led to the village.

The midwife's house was high above the others and in consequence isolated.

Tilda was thankful for that.

It meant it was unlikely that they would be disturbed and as in a small village they doubtless knew the movements of everyone else and once Frau Sturdel was back with her patient everyone would be aware where they could find her.

She bolted the door and crossing the kitchen went into the bedroom.

Rudolph was still asleep.

He looked amazingly handsome and somehow younger with his eyes closed and with the white frill of a nightshirt against his suntanned skin.

Tilda stood looking at him.

How could she have imagined yesterday when she had first seen him in the woods near the *Linderhof* that she would today be here alone with him in a small bungalow without any idea of how she was to return to Munich?

She remembered the passionate demanding kisses he had given Mitzi as they stood together under the silver birch trees.

She felt then he was somehow more exciting and certainly different from any man she had ever seen before.

She remembered how reluctant she had been to leave the woods with the *aide-de-camp*, not knowing who Rudolph and Mitzi were.

Even now she knew little more, although she had taken part in a wild adventure with him and last night she had slept beside him in the same bed!

What would her mother say?

Tilda could almost see the outraged expression on Princess Priscilla's face and hear her exclamations of horror!

Then she began to laugh.

It was so incomprehensible, so unbelievable, and yet so very much more enjoyable than those gloomy Royal Palaces of her disapproving relatives and the sour criticism and grumblings of the Dowager Lady Crewkerne.

'Whatever happens in the future,' Tilda told herself. 'I shall have this to remember. This – and Rudolph!'

Chapter Five

Tilda came back to wakefulness to lie with her eyes closed, letting thoughts drift in and out of her mind.

She remembered first where she was, then she wondered how long they would have to stay in Frau Sturdel's bungalow and how they would go back to Munich when it was safe.

There were so many problems and yet, as she lay half-asleep, they did not seem so insurmountable as they had appeared last night when she had gone to bed.

She felt in some strange way as if she had stepped into another world and another life. She was no longer Lady Victoria Tetherton-Smythe, but was in actual fact Tilda Weber.

She was a person of no consequence and she no longer felt apprehensive about her grand and frightening Royal marriage with a man everyone whispered about.

A slight movement made her open her eyes and she found herself looking directly at Rudolph.

Their faces were only a few inches apart and, as she stared at him, Tilda realised that he too must just have awakened.

There was an expression of sheer astonishment in his eyes and then he said in a low hoarse voice,

"What, are you doing here? What has happened?"

It was, Tilda realised, still very early in the morning and the sunlight coming through the sides of the curtains was very pale.

Then, as she was about to answer Rudolph's questions, she suddenly remembered that she was in bed with him and she was wearing a thin flannel nightgown which Frau Sturdel had brought her last night when she came back to feed the chickens.

"I-I can – explain," she replied hesitantly.

"I remember now." Rudolph said slowly. "I was shot in the leg and you gave me laudanum."

"It was not my – fault you took too – much." Tilda said defensively.

"Too much?" he queried.

"You slept all yesterday," Tilda explained, "It was the night before that we escaped from the Police."

He made a movement as if to turn on his back and gave an exclamation of pain.

"You must be careful," Tilda said hastily. "It is only a flesh wound, but you will find it very painful."

"It *is* painful! "

A little cautiously he raised himself higher on his pillows.

Then he said,

"Would it be an indiscreet question to ask why you are in bed with me?"

Tilda blushed.

Even in the dim light it showed crimson against the whiteness of her skin.

"There was – nowhere else for – me to sleep." she said, "and you were – unconscious."

"I hope you are not thinking that I am ungracious enough to complain," he said with a hint of laughter in his voice.

"Besides," Tilda went on, the words coming out in a rush, "Frau Sturdel thinks we are – married."

"I think you had better start at the beginning," Rudolph said, "and tell me who is Frau Sturdel, although I would guess she is the owner of this house."

"She is the village midwife," Tilda answered, "and that is why I found bandages in her kitchen."

Rudolph put his hand up to his forehead.

"This dope is making me feel extremely stupid," he said. "I suppose it would not be possible for me to have some coffee?"

"I will make you some, if you will shut your eyes," Tilda answered.

"Perhaps you should explain to me why that is essential," Rudolph answered. "As I told you, I am feeling a trifle thick-headed this morning."

"I-I am not – dressed," Tilda faltered in a low voice. "Frau Sturdel brought me a – nightgown and it would have seemed – ungracious not to – wear it."

She paused to continue shyly,

"Besides it was rather – uncomfortable sleeping in – the only clothes I have."

"Your explanations are most plausible," Rudolph said, "and now I understand your predicament I promise you I will close my eyes."

"I will dress in the kitchen," Tilda said, "and then I will bring you some coffee."

She sat up in the bed.

"Your eyes are closed?" she asked anxiously.

"I can see nothing," Rudolph replied.

Tilda slipped out of bed and, picking up her clothes that she had laid on the only chair in the bedroom, she went into the kitchen, closing the door behind her.

The fire in the stove had died down, but she did not have to relight it.

She had brought in a large number of logs from outside before she went to bed, which she now put in the stove.

The flames were soon crackling and she knew that by the time she had washed and dressed the water for the coffee would be boiling in the saucepan.

Cold water from the jug swept what her nurse had always called the 'cobwebs' from her eyes.

Turning, she looked at herself in the small mirror which hung on the wall and combed her hair.

It fell in soft waves on either side of her face and she swept it back from her small ears to let it fall down her back with the few hairpins she had left.

She had lost several running through the woods.

When the coffee was prepared, she poured it into a pretty china coffee pot that matched a large cup and took from the larder a bowl of thick cream that Frau Sturdel had brought back with her yesterday.

She carried it on a tray into the bedroom.

Rudolph had raised himself still further on his pillows and Tilda set the coffee down beside him.

She pulled back the curtains from the window and the sun came streaming in turning her hair to a golden halo.

"I see you are a very proficient housewife," Rudolph remarked. "As we are supposed to be married perhaps you will tell me our name?"

"It is – Weber," Tilda said a little shyly.

He laughed.

"Not very original or distinguished."

"It was the first name that came into my head" Tilda confessed, "and anyway it would be unwise for us to have anything very distinctive, as you well know."

"Have you told our hostess that we are in hiding?"

Tilda nodded.

"She was very kind and sympathetic and I know she will not give us away, but we cannot stay here indefinitely."

"Naturally not," Rudolph answered. "When does she think I will be able to travel?"

"I have not asked her," Tilda said, "but she is a very experienced nurse and when she comes back this morning she will dress your wound. Then she will be able to answer all the questions that are important."

"What is happening in Munich?" he asked.

"Frau Sturdel said last night that there are reports of rioting and the students have actually set some buildings on fire."

"Not a very cheerful prospect for our return."

"I know," Tilda agreed unhappily. "But what will they imagine has – happened to me?"

"Suppose you tell me who *they* are?" Rudolph asked.

He had poured out the coffee and was drinking it while they talked.

Tilda paused and thought quickly.

She would have to be very careful what she said.

"As I told you," she said after a moment, "I was with my – uncle in the Beer Hall. When I took hold of your – hand I thought it was – his."

"And I thought you were someone else," Rudolph smiled.

"Mitzi!" Tilda blurted out involuntarily.

She would have bitten hack the words when she saw the surprise in his eyes, but it was already said.

"Mitzi?" he repeated. "What do you know about Mitzi?"

"I-I saw you arrive while I was waiting for my – uncle to buy the tickets into the Beer Hall," Tilda answered, "and I – heard someone say her – name."

It sounded a lame excuse even to herself, but Rudolph smiled.

"Everyone knows Mitzi," he said, "I am not worried about her. The students will not harm her."

"Who is she?" Tilda asked.

"You don't know?" he enquired.

Tilda shook her head.

"She is the best-known and most popular Music Hall artist in the whole of Bavaria. She is a tremendous draw and has an enormous number of admirers."

Remembering how pretty Mitzi was, Tilda was sure that this was true.

At the same time she could not help feeling humbly that Rudolph would find her a very inadequate substitute for the woman he thought he was saving in the riot.

"She is – very pretty!" she said in a low voice.

"Very!" he agreed. "But we must concern ourselves with your problem. What do you think your uncle will do?"

That was a question she had been asking herself and she had already come to the conclusion that for the moment neither the Professor nor Lady Crewkerne would want to do anything.

It was more than likely that they would just wait and hope she would turn up.

To make enquiries of the Police would be to advertise the fact of her disappearance and the one thing they would wish to avoid would be the scandal of people knowing that she had actually been present at a riot in the Beer Hall.

"I am sure they will be very worried," Rudolph said, "although you still have not explained to me who they are."

"There is my uncle," Tilda said slowly, "and another – relative who is travelling with us."

"And what about your husband?" he asked.

He saw the astonishment in Tilda's eyes and added,

"I see you are wearing a wedding ring."

"No, it is not a wedding ring," Tilda replied, "although I am betrothed."

"To a Bavarian?"

Tilda nodded her head.

This was a safe answer at any rate. Bavaria was a large country.

"And will he not be distraught at your disappearance?"

"He may not – know about it," Tilda said hesitatingly. "He has not yet – arrived in – Munich."

"Tell me about him," Rudolph said. "Are you very much in love?"

"I have not met him!"

There was a moment's silence and then Rudolph repeated almost incredulously,

"You have not met him?"

"No," Tilda answered uncomfortably, "our – marriage has been – arranged."

"I should have thought that was unnecessary."

"Unnecessary?"

"Someone who looks like you must have dozens of suitors, but doubtless this arranged marriage will bring you many advantages."

"I – suppose so," Tilda answered.

Because she was nervous at the way the conversation was developing, she said hastily,

"Let me get you some more coffee. Has what you have drunk cleared your head?"

"I certainly feel a little less of a nitwit," he answered.

"I would get you some breakfast," Tilda told him, "but it seems rather impolite not to wait for Frau Sturdel and I don't like to take the fresh-laid eggs from the hens without asking her permission."

"I can wait," Rudolph replied, "and I am hoping that Frau Sturdel will be able to provide me with a razor. I certainly need a shave."

"I will put some water on to boil," Tilda said. "She should be here at any moment. I am sure she will have her husband's razors hidden away somewhere."

"What has happened to Herr Sturdel whose bed I am undoubtedly occupying?"

"He is dead."

"In which case I can hardly thank him for the loan of his nightshirt," Rudolph said,

"I doubt if he needs it where he has gone," Tilda answered mischievously,

She had her hand on the door into the kitchen when Rudolph asked,

"What is your name? Your real name?"

Again Tilda had to think quickly.

"Hyde," she said, thinking it was appropriate to her present position, "and it is spelt with a 'y'."

"I will not forget that when I write to you," Rudolph said with a twinkle in his eyes.

She laughed as she left him to fill the kettle.

Frau Sturdel hustled in like a fresh wind.

"So you are awake, young man," she said to Rudolph, "and about time too! I was beginning to think that you intended to dream your life away"

"Thanks to you, *meine frau*, I have a comfortable place in which to do so," Rudolph said. "My wife and I are deeply grateful."

Tilda saw that Frau Sturdel was delighted by his courtesy.

'He has a way with women,' she told herself.

Once again she thought of how he had kissed Mitzi amongst the trees and how provocatively she had run away from him, not running so fast that he could not catch her.

"Now you cook the breakfast," Frau Sturdel said to Tilda, "and I will make your husband comfortable."

Tilda could hear them laughing together in the bedroom while Frau Sturdel put fresh bandages on Rudolph's leg and gave him her husband's razors so that he could shave himself.

"You need not worry about that man of yours," she said to Tilda when she had finished. "He's as strong as a horse and the wound is healing nicely. Of course he wants to get up, but I have absolutely forbidden it!"

Tilda looked at her enquiringly and she explained,

"I don't want him to start bleeding again. Young people are always impatient. Leave a wound alone and it will heal itself, that's what I always say."

"Have you heard any news about the rioting?" Tilda enquired.

"My patient's husband works at the Post Office and they, of course, are in communication with the City. They say that things are still bad, but beginning to settle down."

"There have not been any enquiries in the village about us?" Tilda asked anxiously.

"No one knows you are here," Frau Sturdel said reassuringly, "and the Policeman who looks after this village lives two miles away."

Tilda breathed a sigh of relief.

"I brought you some food for your midday meal," Frau Sturdel said. "I expect your husband will be feeling hungry, once the effects of the laudanum have worn off. It is good beef and tender if you cook it slowly."

"I will do that," Tilda promised.

"I will be back this evening. Just keep him quiet. That is all you have to do."

She put on her coat and picked up her shopping basket.

"Take care of him and don't worry. You are not likely to have any callers."

"I hope not," Tilda sighed.

She saw Frau Sturdel off down the path, filled the jug with water from the pump and returned into the house, bolting the door behind her.

She found Rudolph shaved and looking incredibly handsome.

The room was full of sunshine and once again Tilda had the strange feeling that she was in another world and was no longer herself.

"Come and talk to me," Rudolph suggested in his deep voice, "otherwise I shall become bored."

"What do you want to talk about?" Tilda asked nervously.

"About you for one thing," he answered, "I want you to tell me all about your life. This man you are betrothed to, what do you know about him?"

"Very little," Tilda answered truthfully. "My parents think he is a suitable – husband and I really have no – choice in the matter."

"What will happen if you dislike him when you meet?"

Tilda drew in her breath.

She had no idea how expressive her face was, so that Rudolph could see quite clearly that she was not only apprehensive but a little frightened.

"There will be – nothing that I can – do," Tilda said after a moment.

"I think that all *mariages de convenance* are barbaric," he said savagely. "A man and a woman should be allowed to choose their own mate and be permitted to find someone they love before they tie themselves up for life."

He spoke so violently that Tilda asked,

"You are not married?"

"No."

"Why not?"

"There are a number of reasons," he answered, "but principally because a man has much more fun when he is a bachelor."

"Fun?" Tilda asked and then she added, "You mean they can enjoy themselves with lots of women rather than being faithful to one?"

"I should say that pretty well sums it up," Rudolph agreed.

"Do you want – would you like to – marry Mitzi?" Tilda asked.

"Good Lord, *no!*"

He spoke spontaneously and Tilda felt a sudden gladness within her that had not been there before.

"Why not?" she asked.

He hesitated a moment before he answered,

"One does not marry the Mitzis of this world, alluring and attractive though they may be."

"But you like being with her?"

Rudolph looked at her searchingly before he replied,

"Are you not insinuating rather a lot just because you saw Mitzi and me going into the Beer Hall? We were simply having supper together."

Tilda did not answer and then he demanded,

"What are you thinking about? What are you assuming?"

"I don't think I am – assuming anything," Tilda answered. "I am just trying to understand. I have never seen anyone before – who looked like Mitzi."

"I suppose not," Rudolph said in a voice as if he was thinking about something else.

Then he said,

"I can imagine your life in England has been fairly restricted. Surely it was out of character for you to go to a Beer Hall?"

"I – persuaded my – uncle to take me there – " Tilda said.

"I suppose you coaxed him into it and he did not like to refuse," Rudolph remarked. "At the same time the English are usually too stuffy to enjoy such places."

"It seemed very gay and I was enjoying myself until the students broke in."

"Who could have imagined that things would get so rough?" Rudolph ruminated, "or that we would find ourselves in the predicament we are in at the moment."

"You don't think the Police are still searching for us?"

"We can only hope not," he answered. "They will have recovered their wagon by now and we can only pray that they will forget the whole episode."

There was a doubtful note in his voice that did not escape Tilda.

"And supposing they do go on looking for us?"

"We have already extricated ourselves from several uncomfortable situations. It will merely mean that we will have to extricate ourselves from one more!"

Tilda smiled.

"You were very clever the way you managed to avoid us being taken to the Police Station for – "

"For an interrogation!" Rudolph finished.

Tilda was silent for a moment and then she asked,

"It may seem – impertinent, in which case you can – refuse to answer me, but what have you – done?"

Her blue eyes were very curious and Rudolph looked at her for a long moment before he said,

"What have you been imagining? That I am a bank robber, a jewel thief or perhaps an anarchist?"

"No, of course not," Tilda said, "none of those things, but I could not help wondering why you are hiding from the Police.

"Perhaps my worst offence is being absent without leave," Rudolph said slowly.

"You are a soldier?"

He nodded his head.

"But not a deserter?"

"No, of course not," he replied. "I am merely playing truant. Something that is frowned upon by the powers that be!"

'That is just what I was doing,' Tilda thought to herself.

At the same time she could not help feeling relieved that Rudolph's crimes were not worse.

She had been worried in the night in case she had allied herself to someone thoroughly despicable – someone who, if he were discovered, would involve her in even more scandal than she was in already.

It had seemed impossible that Rudolph could be a criminal and yet, Tilda told herself, one could never be certain.

It was obvious that a clever experienced crook would not look like one, unlike 'toughs' who wanted to look more ferocious than they really were.

But being absent without leave, although it might involve a stiff sentence in the Army, was not something that would concern the civilian Police, although doubtless there was a liaison between the two.

She realised suddenly that Rudolph was watching her.

"Well?" he asked, "are you glad it is nothing more violent? You might have entrusted yourself to a murderer or a strangler!"

"Of course I did not think you were anything like that," Tilda replied almost hotly.

"As it happens, I don't think that either of us had time to think of anything but saving our skins," Rudolph said.

He laughed.

"I wish I could have seen the faces of those Policemen in the square when they saw their wagon disappearing before their very eyes. It will teach them to be more careful in the future."

"They have had their revenge by shooting you in the leg"

"It was entirely my own fault," he sighed. "If I had not forgotten that there would be barricades across the roads, we could have stopped sooner and perhaps turned down some country lane where no one would have found us."

"We have been lucky as it is," Tilda said. "Very lucky!"

"I agree," he said, "very lucky!"

His eyes were on her face.

Tilda cooked their luncheon and Rudolph commended her skill.

"Your future husband will certainly not have to complain about how you feed him," he pointed out.

Thinking of the dull rather stodgy food that she had eaten with her relatives coming through Europe, Tilda wondered if she would have any chance of improving the *cuisine* in the Palace in Obernia.

She was well aware that it would not be protocol for her to interfere and then she told herself that, as Prince Maximilian was young compared with her Royal relatives, he would surely not be so hidebound or stuffy in his ways as they were.

"What are you thinking about?" Rudolph asked unexpectedly, "You look worried."

"I was thinking about my future," Tilda replied.

"That worries you?"

"Yes, of course it does. How would you like to be told you had to marry somebody without having seen her or knowing what she was like?"

Rudolph did not answer for a moment and then he asked,

"I presume that what you are bringing to the marriage is money and he is contributing rank?"

Tilda could see that this sort of conversation was dangerous.

She started to clear away the plates and dishes that Rudolph had eaten his luncheon from.

She took them into the kitchen, washed them up and then thought that he might take this opportunity to have a little nap.

But, when she entered the bedroom, she knew that he had been waiting for her as his eyes were watching the door.

"Come here, Tilda!" he said. "I want to talk to you."

"About what?" she asked.

"Come and sit on the bed beside me."

She obeyed him sitting down on the edge of the mattress so that she was facing him.

He took her hand in his.

"You are so small and lovely," he said, "that I cannot bear to think of you being unhappy."

Tilda looked at him in astonishment.

No one had ever spoken to her before in quite that gentle and caressing manner which seemed to send a little thrill through her.

She was also vividly conscious of the strength of his fingers as they held hers.

"It is not only that," Rudolph said. "I am worried in case being here with me should get you into trouble. When your people learn about it, they will doubtless think it wrong and very reprehensible."

"Perhaps they will never – know," Tilda stammered.

"We must hope we can keep it a secret," he answered. "But after I leave you in Munich, you will have to offer some explanation as to what you have been doing from the time they lost you to the time you return."

"I expect I shall think of something," Tilda said.

It was difficult at the moment to think of anything but the fact that she was close to him and he was touching her.

"We will talk it over when the time comes," Rudolph said. "In the meantime we will continue to play husband and wife. I congratulate myself on the fact that, although it all happened in the dark, I chose a very alluring bride!"

"And you are the most handsome man I have ever seen."

"Thank you," he answered, "but I have the feeling that you should not be so generous with your compliments."

"You mean – it was wrong for me to say that I think you are – handsome?"

"Not wrong," he said, "but it is something you would never have said to an Englishman."

Tilda gave a little giggle.

"No indeed, but then I have never seen one who is as good-looking as you."

Rudolph's fingers tightened on hers.

"You are adorable!" he said. "I expect many men have told you that?"

"No one has ever said anything I really wanted to hear," Tilda admitted. "Do you really think – that?"

"That you are adorable?" he asked. "But of course! I never imagined that an English girl could be so small, so exquisite! In fact, little Tilda, you look like something out of a Fairytale."

"That is lovely!" Tilda said. "You do say charming things! Do you say them to all the women you meet, like Mitzi?"

"You also ask the most embarrassing questions!" Rudolph exclaimed. "Somehow I cannot imagine the type of English household you have been brought up in."

"Perhaps because of the way I have been brought up I now feel that I can say what I think."

She gave a little sigh.

"It is so dull, so terribly dull to have to keep thinking before you speak."

"I have found that too," Rudolph agreed. "But you ought not to find life dull at your age. Now let me guess – "

He paused for a moment to go on,

" – if you were in England at this moment you would be driving in Hyde Park. You might visit the Crystal Palace and you would be partnered at a ball tonight by smart young gentlemen wearing stiff white shirt-fronts and white gloves."

Tilda laughed.

"How do you know all that about England?"

"I have been in England during what is called the 'London Season'," Rudolph answered, "and I have watched the *debutantes*, who looked like you but were not nearly so pretty, step out of their carriages closely chaperoned by fierce-looking Dowagers as they trotted into some impressive house to take part in the 'marriage market'."

"The 'marriage market'!" Tilda exclaimed.

"What else is it?" Rudolph asked. "When girls born into a certain stratum of Society must hope to entice into matrimony the highest bidder. In other words the man with the most money or the grandest-sounding title."

There was a note of scorn in Rudolph's voice, which made Tilda feel uncomfortable.

Although it had not happened to her, she was quite certain that what he said was true.

The *debutantes* who went to the balls night after night were in a kind of 'marriage market' and their only ambition was to win an important husband either as regards rank or wealth.

"Well, this is all experience for you," Rudolph said. "Doubtless you will marry your important Bavarian and strive to forget the impropriety of sharing a wooden hut on the mountainside alone with me."

"It is an adventure," Tilda said in a low voice, "and I shall never – forget it."

"Are you sure about that?"

"Quite – quite sure."

But for some reason Tilda did not understand she found it hard to look into his eyes.

They talked all through the afternoon.

They both liked music and Rudolph described the enormous success Wagner had achieved in Bavaria.

They had both read many of the same authors and were intrigued by Darwin's Theory of Evolution.

While they found that they had so much in common, Tilda had the feeling that they were in a way duelling with each other.

She was concealing secrets from Rudolph and she thought that he too had secrets he was keeping from her.

She wondered if they concerned Mitzi, but she was sure that he was far too clever to tell her anything he did not wish her to know.

She on the other hand was terrified of making a slip, of being too revealing, because she was quite certain that it would not escape his notice!

Yet never, she told herself, had she enjoyed an afternoon more.

It was incredible to think that this was the first time she had ever been alone with a man and a young man at that.

Always before there had been her mother to chaperone her or someone old and authoritative to take her mother's place.

But even so, chaperoned or not, she had never had the opportunity of talking to a man like Rudolph.

She could not have believed a man could be so handsome and yet so extremely masculine.

There was nothing soft or effete about him and she had a feeling, which she could not explain that he was very experienced with women.

It was quite a surprise when Frau Sturdel returned to find that it was six o'clock.

"I don't suppose you missed me!" she remarked with a smile, "but I have been wondering how my patient is getting on."

"I am completely recovered!" Rudolph answered.

"That's for me to say," Frau Sturdel insisted.

She got everything ready to change the bandages on his leg and then gave Tilda a number of tasks that took her out into the garden or kept her in the kitchen.

Tilda had the idea that Rudolph had asked Frau Sturdel to keep her away while she attended to him.

'If he thinks his wound will upset me, he is mistaken!' Tilda told herself proudly.

Equally she was rather glad she did not have to look at it again.

She had not forgotten how frightening it had seemed that first night when she had tried to staunch the flow of blood and being afraid that she would not know how to do so.

Frau Sturdel brought them some roe deer steaks for dinner and Rudolph pronounced them excellent!

She also had a bottle of beer for him in her basket and, when he thanked her for her thoughtfulness, she answered,

"I am not so old that I have forgotten what a man enjoys!"

"Why have you not married again?" Rudolph asked her.

"I've found no one who took my fancy and that's the truth!" Frau Sturdel said.

"I bet every man in the village is ready to lay his heart at your feet," Rudolph remarked.

"Get along with you!" Frau Sturdel laughed, but she was obviously delighted at the compliment and looked quite coy.

"I must go back," she said when they had finished their supper.

"Has the baby not been born yet?" Tilda asked.

"It is still keeping us waiting," Frau Sturdel answered, "and that's why I am quite certain it's a girl!"

She set off again for the village.

Tilda locked the door and came back rather slowly into the bedroom.

Rudolph looked at her for a long moment and then he said,

"What is worrying you now?"

"I am – wondering where I can – sleep tonight," she answered.

"Where you slept last night!"

She blushed.

"I think it would be – wrong now that you are conscious although I don't quite know why it – should be."

There was a pause before Rudolph said,

"I could give you a number of reasons, but actually I have a solution,"

"You have?"

"When I was in Sweden," he said, "they told me of a strange custom that is enjoyed by engaged couples."

"What is that?" Tilda asked.

"As you know, it is very cold there in the winter and there is usually a stove only in the main sitting room," Rudolph began. "So if the engaged couple want to talk to each other alone, and it is far too cold for them to be in a separate room without a fire, they get into bed together."

"Into bed!" Tilda exclaimed.

"Yes," he answered, "but a large bolster is put down the middle of the bed between them so that they cannot touch each other. The custom is called 'bundling'."

"It sounds rather strange," Tilda remarked.

"Strange or not, it is the answer to our present problem. You can take away the bolster I have been lying on. And then if you put it in the centre of the bed it will, I promise you, prove a most effective chaperone!"

"It sounds – sensible," Tilda said.

"It is sensible," he answered. "I could, of course, roll myself onto the floor, which would be exceedingly uncomfortable, or you could sit bolt upright on the hard chair, but there is no other alternative."

"There is not," Tilda agreed, "and so we will 'bundle' if that is the right word! "

She put the bolster down the centre of the bed and then she said,

"I will undress in the kitchen, but will you shut your eyes as you did this morning?"

"I will."

"You promise?"

"Soldier's honour!"

"I don't think that sounds very convincing. Who is your Patron Saint of Obernia?"

"There are a number of them," Rudolph replied. "St. Gerhardt is, I suppose, one of the most popular."

"I have never heard of him," Tilda said. "What did he do?"

"He started off rather well," Rudolph answered, "by killing a few dragons and winning the hand of a Princess. Then he deteriorated."

"In what way?"

"He left his castle, his wife and his children, and roamed about the country in a monk's robe trying to find pieces of the True Cross."

"I suppose he wanted to be holy?"

"I call it a very easy excuse for renouncing your responsibilities," Rudolph remarked. "But I will swear on St. Gerhardt, if it pleases you."

"We have to impose a penalty in case you break your vow," Tilda teased him.

"What do you suggest?"

"What would you hate to lose or give up most?"

He thought for a moment and then he said with a twinkle in his eyes,

"I suppose the answer to that is 'wine, women and song', although I am not too particular about the song!"

"Very well. Now you must repeat after me,

> *'St. Gerhardt, if I tell a lie,*
> *No wine or women till I die'.*"

"That is far too stringent!" Rudolph protested.

"Then what do you suggest?"

He thought for a moment and then he said slowly,

> *"St. Gerhardt, if I tell a lie,*
> *Give me only one woman till I die."*

"I should have thought that was nearly as bad," Tilda said. "It would mean you would have to be married and there would be no more Mitzis and no more gay amusing supper parties. You would just have to sit at home with your wife!"

She laughed and then unexpectedly her eyes were held by Rudolph's and the laughter died on her lips.

She did not know why, but for the moment it was impossible to move, impossible to breathe.

"It would depend who I married!" Rudolph said in his deep voice.

Chapter Six

Tilda was helping Frau Sturdel wash up the breakfast things.

They were a little later than before, as they had sat talking and laughing with Rudolph.

"I think the baby will arrive this morning," Frau Sturdel was saying.

"Are you sure?" Tilda enquired.

"As sure as one can be of anything in this wicked world," Frau Sturdel replied. "But babies are always unpredictable."

Tilda smiled.

She put down the plate she had dried and then, glancing out of the window, let out a frightened gasp.

"Frau Sturdel!" she called out in an urgent tone.

"What is it?"

"Look!"

Below the bungalow they could see two Policemen in uniform climbing slowly towards them.

"That is our local Constable and another," Frau Sturdel said.

"What shall we do? Where can we hide?" Tilda asked nervously.

Frau Sturdel crossed the kitchen and slipped the bolt into place on the door.

Then she said to Tilda,

"Quick! Into the bedroom!"

Tilda obeyed and Rudolph looked up in surprise as they both entered.

"There are two Policemen coming here," Tilda explained in a low voice.

Frau Sturdel went to the wardrobe that stood on one wall of the bedroom.

"Get into the centre of the bed, both of you," she ordered.

Tilda looked at her in surprise, but Rudolph moved a little from the side and Tilda, after a moment's hesitation, lifted the *düchent* and lay down beside him.

She was not quite certain what Frau Sturdel intended, but she felt terrified that they might both be taken away for interrogation at the Police Station.

From a shelf on top of the wardrobe Frau Sturdel took down a heavy cover, which Tilda knew in England was called a 'patchwork quilt'.

Tiny pieces of different coloured materials were joined together to make an extremely intricate and pretty bed cover.

But there was no time to notice anything!

She lay straight out beside Rudolph and he put his arm around her.

She quivered and felt a moment's embarrassment, because she had never been so close to a man before.

Frau Sturdel was covering them with her patchwork quilt.

As she did so, Tilda realised that the fact that they were in the centre of the bed would be concealed by the *düchent*, which would only appear more buoyant and puffy than usual.

Otherwise, when they were completely covered, there would be no reason to suspect that the bed was occupied.

As if he understood Frau Sturdel's intentions, Rudolph separated the two pillows so that his head and Tilda's were in a space between them.

Then, even as Frau Sturdel covered them completely, there was a knock at the door.

"Keep very still!" she whispered.

She went from the room and across the kitchen.

She left the bedroom door ajar, as if she had nothing to hide.

Rudolph and Tilda could hear her pull back the bolt and say in a tone of surprise,

"*Guten morgen, Herr Oberinspektor!*"

"*Guten morgen,* Frau Sturdel!" a man's voice replied.

"You wish to see me?" Frau Sturdel asked.

"Yes, indeed," the Constable answered, "and I have brought with me my superior, *Herr Oberpolizei-Inspektor.*"

"*Guten morgen, mein herr!*" Frau Sturdel said. "Will you come in and can I make you a cup of coffee?"

"It is kind of you, Frau Sturdel, but we have no time," the Constable replied. "*Herr Oberpolizei-Inspektor* wishes to ask you a question."

"And what can that be?" Frau Sturdel enquired.

"I am making enquiries," *Herr Oberpolizei-Inspektor* said, "about two students who three nights ago stole a Police wagon in Munich."

"A Police wagon?" Frau Sturdel ejaculated. "That was a strange thing to do!"

"They were escaping," *Herr Oberpolizei-Inspektor* said firmly, "It was a disgraceful thing to happen and the Police concerned have been severely reprimanded!"

"I can understand that," Frau Sturdel said, "but I can assure you, *mein herr*, there is no Police wagon in this village."

"The Police wagon has been recovered," *Herr Oberpolizei-Inspektor* replied, "but the students escaped!"

"We are a long way from Munich, *mein herr.*"

'They were last seen climbing the hills to the West of here." *Herr Oberpolizei-Inspektor* answered. "Shots were fired in their direction, although it is doubtful if they were hit."

"If they were not," Frau Sturdel said, "I should imagine that they are far away by this time."

"That is exactly what I said," the Constable interposed, "but *Herr Oberpolizei-Inspektor* insists on asking you if you have any knowledge of these young people."

"Two men?" Frau Sturdel asked.

"The Policemen who fired at them thought, although then were not certain, that it was a man and a woman, but I can see, Frau Sturdel, that you cannot help us in this matter."

"I am afraid not," Frau Sturdel said with a little sigh, "but if I can I will, of course, get in touch with *Herr Oberinspektor*, unless – "

She paused for a moment.

" – Unless you want to search my house? As you see it is not very large and it would be difficult to hide anyone here."

"I can see that!" *Herr Oberpolizei-Inspektor* said, "and you must forgive us for worrying you when I know you are busy with a confinement."

"I am indeed," Frau Sturdel said, "and it has been a long wait for a baby who seems most reluctant to enter the world. I cannot think why!"

"Perhaps he has no wish to become a rioting student!" the Constable suggested and laughed heartily at his own joke.

"You always were a wit, *Herr Oberinspektor*!" Frau Sturdel exclaimed. "But if I was a betting woman, I would like to wager on this baby being a girl!"

"We must not take up any more of your time, *meine frau*," *Herr Oberpolizei-Inspektor* said coldly as if he thought that such exchanges of pleasantry were a waste of time. "I will make enquiries of the Priest to see if he can help us and afterwards I must go on to the next village."

"I hope you will be more successful there than you have been here, *mein herr*," Frau Sturdel said.

"Thank you," *Herr Oberpolizei-Inspektor* replied politely. "*Guten morgen*, Frau Sturde*l*"

"*Guten morgen, Herr Oberpolizei-Inspektor. Guten morgen, Herr Oberinspektor.*"

The exchange of pleasantries seemed to go on forever.

Tilda, who had been lying rigid with her face against Rudolph's shoulder, felt herself relax.

The Police were leaving and they were safe!

She knew that Rudolph had been tense too.

Neither of them had moved a muscle since Frau Sturdel had covered them with the patchwork quilt.

Now Rudolph's arm tightened around her.

They heard Frau Sturdel close the door and Tilda let out her breath with a deep sigh that seemed to come from her heart.

"Once again we have escaped!" she said in a whisper raising her face in the darkness towards Rudolph.

He must have looked down at her at the same moment because unexpectedly his mouth was on hers.

For a moment Tilda was conscious of nothing but surprise and then his lips gave her a strange incredible ecstasy.

It was as if a shaft of lightning shot through her and she knew that this was what she had been really wanting.

This was what she had been yearning for ever since she had seen him kissing Mitzi in the woods near the *Linderhof.*

She had tried to imagine what they had felt, but the reality was so different, so unbelievably wonderful, that her lips could only cling to his.

In that moment she forgot the danger they had been in, the heavy darkness of the quilt covering them!

There was no one else in the world except themselves.

It was almost a physical pain to take her lips from his as Frau Sturdel folded back the quilt.

"That was a near shave!" she exclaimed. "I was half-afraid that our local Constable, who is always nosy, would inspect the wardrobe and find your clothes hanging up in it."

She took the cover off them and for a moment Tilda realised that it was impossible to move.

She wanted to stay where she was with her head on Rudolph's shoulder and his face very close to hers.

Then he took his arm from her and she was free.

Automatically, hardly aware of what she was doing. Tilda climbed from the bed to help Frau Sturdel fold up the quilt.

She put it back in its place on top of the wardrobe.

"I never thought when my grandmother gave me this that it would prove so useful!" Frau Sturdel was saying.

"We can only say how deeply grateful we are," Rudolph told her.

"After all the trouble I have had with you." Frau Sturdel said with a smile. "I was not going to hand you over to the Police!"

"How can we possibly express our thanks?" Rudolph asked.

"By keeping me out of the sort of trouble you are in!" Frau Sturdel retorted.

She glanced at the door and said,

"I must hurry back or they will be coming up the hill to find out what has happened to me. I will be home this evening at the usual time. Goodbye, children."

She walked into the kitchen and paused.

"Frau Weber," she said, "you must put the meat I brought you for your luncheon in the larder, otherwise the flies will be on it."

"I will do that," Tilda said.

Her voice sounded a little unsteady even to herself, but she followed Frau Sturdel into the kitchen, obediently putting the meat in the small larder, which was protected by close netting from bluebottles and other flies.

By the time she had finished, Frau Sturdel was already halfway down the hill.

Tilda went back into the bedroom.

Rudolph was sitting up in his usual manner against the pillows.

As their eyes met, she stood for a moment gazing at him, her face radiant before she ran forward, holding out her hands towards him.

"Rudolph! *Rudolph*," she whispered.

She wanted, as she had never wanted anything in her life, for him to kiss her again.

She would have thrown herself into his arms, but he checked her and somehow she found herself sitting on the side of the bed facing him as she had done before.

"It was a mistake, Tilda," he said in a low voice. "You have to forget it."

"Forget that you – kissed me?" Tilda asked.

"Yes."

"But it was wonderful! The most wonderful thing that has ever – happened to me. Why should I – forget it?"

He did not answer and after a moment she said in a small, lost little voice,

"You mean – you did not – like kissing – me?"

"No, of course I don't mean that," Rudolph exclaimed. "It was marvellous! The most perfect kiss I have ever known, but Tilda, it must not happen again,"

"Why – not?" Tilda asked. "I don't – understand."

He took one of her hands in both of his and looked down at it and Tilda knew that he was feeling for words.

"Listen to me, Tilda," he said, "we met by chance. We can mean nothing to each other in the future and I would not wish to hurt you."

"But why should you – hurt me?" Tilda asked.

He did not answer and after a moment she said in a whisper,

"I – want you to – kiss me again."

"Tilda, try to be sensible."

"Why should it matter?" Tilda asked. "No one would know any more than they will know – that we have slept together in the same bed."

"It is not as easy as that."

"Why not? I don't – understand. You kiss – other women. Why not – me?"

"I will give you two reasons," Rudolph replied.

"What are they?" Tilda enquired.

"The first is because you are a lady."

Tilda wanted to argue about this! To argue that an accident of birth should not be an obstacle to his kissing her!

But Rudolph went on,

"Have you ever been inside a Bavarian Church?"

Tilda looked at him in surprise and replied,

"Yes, of course. We stopped at lots of Churches on our way through Bavaria. They are beautiful! More beautiful than any other Churches I have ever seen."

"Did you look at the carvings?" Rudolph asked, "and did you notice the angels?"

"But of course," Tilda answered, "there were angels everywhere, lovely, exquisite, happy little angels dancing above the pulpit, behind the altar and painted on the ceilings."

"That is what you look like," Rudolph said, "a small, lovely, exquisite little angel!"

There was a depth in his voice that made Tilda gaze at him wide-eyed.

After a moment's pause he said,

"No man who was worthy of the name could hurt anything so perfect, so unbelievably lovely."

"Am I really – like that?" Tilda whispered.

"I never knew anyone could be so absolutely beautiful!" Rudolph said softly.

"And I have never seen – anyone so handsome. You said I ought not to tell you so – but I don't see why I should not do so – any more than I still don't understand why – feeling as you do – you will not kiss me again."

"That is what I am trying to explain to you," Rudolph persisted.

He gave a deep sigh.

"We have our separate ways to go. You are betrothed and we live in different worlds from one another. After you go back to Munich, you will never see me again."

His words gave Tilda a sharp pain in her breast. It was as if he had thrown a knife into her body.

Her fingers tightened on his and she said,

"But I want to – see you. I want to go – on being with – you."

"I want it too," Rudolph replied, "but it is impossible!"

There was silence and he did not look at her.

After a moment Tilda said hesitatingly,

"If – if we really have to – leave each other, could we not be – happy while we are – together? P-Please, Rudolph – please – kiss me again!"

"I have told you *no*," he said sharply and his voice sounded raw. "You must not drive me too hard, Tilda. I am a man, but I am trying to behave decently as you would expect of a gentleman."

"I still don't – understand why it would matter if you – kissed me again," Tilda said.

"One day you will understand," Rudolph said in a deep voice. "Your husband will doubtless explain it to you."

Tilda snatched her hand from between his and said crossly,

"Now you are talking like Mama! I am sick and tired of people refusing to answer my questions – saying that my husband will tell me this – my husband will tell me that! Supposing he does not?"

"What did your mother say to you?" Rudolph asked.

Tilda looked away from him towards the window.

"I asked Mama," she said in a low voice, "what – happens when a man – sleeps in the same – bed with – his wife."

"What did she tell you?"

"She said that my husband would explain all that to me. Then she added – something I did not – follow."

"What was that?" Rudolph asked.

"She said, 'your husband may do things that you think unpleasant, but remember – as his wife, you must obey him. It is – the will of God'."

Tilda's voice faltered away into silence and then she said,

"What will he – do?"

Rudolph did not answer and she went on,

"I cannot think why everybody should be so mysterious and secretive – about – love and about the – man I am to marry."

Rudolph drew a deep breath.

"You are so young, so very young, my sweet. It is difficult for me to help you, in fact I must *not* help you."

"Why not?" Tilda asked crossly. "What are these secrets I cannot be told?"

Rudolph did not answer.

He was watching her face. Her blue eyes were worried and there was a pout to her lips.

'I am right,' he thought, 'she looks exactly like a small, rather unhappy little angel.'

There was something ethereal and spiritual about Tilda, yet despite her child-like appearance there was also something very feminine and alluring.

She stood up from the bed.

"Very well" she said coldly, "If you will not tell me what I want to know. I expect that I shall find someone sooner or later who will do so. I shall just go on – asking until I am given an – answer!"

"You will get one from your husband," Rudolph said and his voice was harsh.

"I doubt it" Tilda snapped. "I expect he will be like the rest of you, saying I am too young, too stupid, too pretty, too ugly, too tall, too short, in fact any excuse to avoid telling me the truth. I did not know that men were so – insensitive."

Rudolph smiled as if he could not help himself.

"You sound exactly like a small kitten spitting at a bull terrier! I have the feeling that you have known very few men."

"I thought you were different from the men I have met," Tilda said, thinking of her pompous relations.

"I am afraid I have disappointed you."

"You – *have*!"

She walked away as she spoke into the kitchen.

She was finding it hard to believe that Rudolph really would not kiss her again, would not give her that marvellous rapturous feeling that had seeped through her body, setting it aglow when his lips had held hers.

She gave a little sigh.

'So that is what a kiss is like!' she thought. 'At least I shall have something to – remember when I never – see him – again!'

The idea hurt her, but telling herself that she would not let him know it, she picked up the empty jug and walked across the kitchen to the door.

She opened the door and stood still.

Outside, obviously just about to knock at the door, was a resplendent-looking Army Officer.

Behind him was a soldier holding the bridles of two horses.

"*Guten morgen!*" the Officer began.

Frightened, Tilda took a quick glance over her shoulder.

She was thankful to see that, when she had left the bedroom, she had not left the door open.

She had meant to slam it because she was angry, but it was not completely closed, although it was impossible to see into the room.

"What do – you want?" she asked in a trembling voice.

"I have no wish to alarm you," the Officer answered.

He glanced at her hand and seeing what he thought was a wedding ring added, *"miene frau."*

Tilda found it difficult to speak and he went on,

"Could I talk to you for a moment? I will not keep you long."

With a great effort Tilda recovered her composure.

"Of course, *Herr Lieutenant*," she replied noticing the insignia on his shoulder.

"May I come in, *meine frau?*" the Lieutenant suggested.

"It would be an honour, *Herr Lieutenant.*"

Tilda was thinking quickly.

This Officer, she thought, is obviously looking for Rudolph.

He had said that he was absent without leave.

These soldiers were trying to arrest him and return him to his Regiment, when he would be tried and punished.

'I must save him! *I must save him!*' she thought to herself.

She crossed the small kitchen to put the jug down by the sink, which gave her time to think,

She decided that she must be pleasant, very charming and convince the Officer that she knew nothing.

The Lieutenant was standing in the centre of the small kitchen dragging off his gloves.

"You have a cosy little house here, *meine frau.*"

"It does not belong to me," Tilda answered, "but to my mother-in-law. My husband and I are – staying with her."

"Your husband is here?"

"Not at the moment," Tilda answered.

"Then I would like to talk to you."

"But of course," she smiled. "Will you not seat yourself?"

She indicated the chair that would ensure that he had his back to the bedroom door.

"Thank you," he said.

"May I make you some coffee, *Herr Lieutenant?*"

"No, thank you, but it is kind of you to suggest it. What is your name?"

"Frau Weber."

Tilda seated herself on the other chair and the table was between them.

The Lieutenant was good-looking, she decided, with curly fair hair, somewhat pronounced features and grey-blue eyes that, she realised, were looking at her with a glint in them.

She raised her eyes to his and asked softly,

"How can I help you? I am only too willing to do what I can."

"You are very kind, *meine frau.*"

"I will try to be," Tilda said, "if you will explain what you want."

"I am trying to discover if anyone in this village has seen a young man in Bavarian dress," the Lieutenant answered.

"There are lots of young men," Tilda replied with a smile, "wearing Bavarian dress."

"Yes, I know that," the Lieutenant said. "I am explaining myself rather badly. This man, who was last seen near the *Linderhof*, is exceptionally handsome. I think if you had seen him you would have noticed him."

"Is he as good-looking as you?" Tilda asked admiringly.

"You flatter me, *meine frau*! He is a great deal better looking! "

"I cannot believe – it is possible!" Tilda said in child-like surprise, "but then the men in this part of Europe are all handsome. I feel I shall never be able to look at – another Englishman."

"I thought you must be English," the Lieutenant said, "and if as you say, *meine frau*, some of our men are handsome, there are no women as beautiful or as attractive as the English."

Tilda smiled at him beguilingly.

"Thank you," she said, "I know you are only flattering me – but I like being flattered."

"I am sure there are hundreds of men willing to do that," the Lieutenant said with a sudden depth in his voice.

Tilda looked away from him rather shyly.

"I suggest – " the Lieutenant began and then stopped.

"What were you going to say?" Tilda enquired.

"If you will not think it impertinent," he said. "I was just wondering if it would be possible for you to dine with me one evening? There is a very good inn not far from here. It is called *The Royal Boundary*."

Tilda looked down in what she hoped was a coy manner.

"It is very kind of you. *Herr Lieutenant*," she said, "and I would like it very much, but my husband would disapprove."

"How long are you staying here?" he enquired.

"My husband leaves at the end of next week, but I shall be staying on for a little while longer."

There was a pause and then the Lieutenant said,

"In which case do you think I might call again to see you?"

"I cannot – prevent you coming here, *mein herr*."

"Then I will call," the Lieutenant said, "and please, *meine frau*, be a little kind to a lonely soldier."

"I cannot believe there are not many – women ready to make – sure that you are not – lonely, *Herr Lieutenant*."

"But, *meine frau*, they do not look like you."

He rose with some reluctance to his feet.

"I must continue with my enquiries," he said. "I will call next week to enquire whether you have seen this handsome young man of whom I speak and also to ask you if you will dine with me,"

"You have not told me the name of the man you are seeking," Tilda said.

"His friends call him 'Rudolph'," the Lieutenant said. "His other name is immaterial. He may have changed it. Actually he is an Obernian."

"I will look out for him." Tilda assured him.

"How can I thank you for being so kind or so beautiful?" the Lieutenant asked.

As he spoke, he took Tilda's hand in his and raised it to his mouth. His lips were warm and hard on her skin.

"I shall be counting the hours," he said, "until the end of next week. *Auf wiedersehen, meine frau*."

"*Auf wiedersehen, Herr Lieutenant*."

He saluted smartly and she stood in the doorway as he mounted his horse.

He saluted her again before he rode away taking the track back into the woods through which he must have come.

Tilda closed the door and bolted it.

She stood for a moment with a smile on her lips.

"Tilda!"

The call from the bedroom was authoritative.

She walked across the kitchen to throw open the door.

"Was I not clever?" she asked.

"Come here!"

Obediently she moved towards Rudolph only to realise as she neared the side of the bed that he was scowling and looked angrier than any man she had ever seen before.

He reached out to grip her wrist.

"How dare you!" he stormed. "How dare you behave in that fast flirtatious manner with that damned Lieutenant?"

"He was enquiring – for you!" Tilda retorted. "He might have searched the house if I had not been pleasant to him."

"Pleasant? You call that pleasant?" Rudolph asked furiously.

Suddenly he pulled her violently into his arms.

"Tilda! *Tilda!*" he cried hoarsely and his lips were once again on hers.

He kissed her fiercely and passionately, his mouth holding her captive.

At first she felt only pain, then, as a rapture streaked through her and the ecstasy she had known before rose within her breasts, Rudolph raised his head to say,

"You are mine! Do you hear me? You are mine and I cannot lose you."

There was no chance for Tilda to reply, for now he was kissing her wildly, kissing her with hard, demanding, angry kisses, which were half-pain and half a wonder beyond words.

She felt herself quiver and tremble in his arms.

Then the room seemed to whirl around her and she became a part of him and his wild burning kisses aroused an echoing fire in her.

Gradually Tilda realised that Rudolph was no longer angry.

Instead he was kissing her slowly and possessively in a manner that seemed to make her a part of him, so that she no longer had any will or identity of her own.

She was his!

His voice when he spoke again seemed only to echo what she already knew without words.

"You are mine! You belong to me!" he said, "and I know now my precious, that I cannot live without you – !"

*

A long time later Tilda murmured shyly,

"I – love – you!"

"And I love you, my little angel," Rudolph replied. "So we have to make plans."

"What plans?" Tilda asked.

He gave a deep sigh.

"It is not going to be easy to do what we want to do."

"I want you to go on – kissing me," Tilda whispered.

"I want that too, my precious," Rudolph replied, "but we have to think a little further ahead."

"Why?"

He smiled.

"Because, although at the moment this place is like Heaven, we cannot stay here for the rest of our lives."

Even as he spoke, Tilda thought of Lady Crewkerne and the Professor waiting for her in Munich, of Prince Maximilian making preparations for their marriage, of the Queen in Windsor Castle thinking of her as an Ambassador for England.

She gave a little cry.

"Nothing matters but – you! They cannot make me marry – someone I do not – love."

"You must free yourself from your engagement," Rudolph demanded. "It will be hard for you, my darling, but you will have to be firm."

"I will not – marry him!"

"I will not let you do so," he answered, tightening his arms around her.

"Could we not just – run away together?" Tilda asked. Rudolph shook his head.

"You are under age, my lovely one. Your parents or Guardians could force you by law to return to them and there would be nothing we could do about it."

Tilda put her arms round his neck.

"I cannot give you – up."

"Nor do I intend that you shall," Rudolph said in his deep voice. "I will marry you whatever difficulties, whatever obstacles people try to put in our way."

He kissed her forehead before he proclaimed,

"I know now there could be no happiness for me in the world unless I can have you."

"When did you first love me?" Tilda asked.

"When I awoke to see your exquisite little face on the pillow," he answered. "I thought I must be dreaming. I could not believe anyone could look so lovely, so unbelievably adorable!"

"Do you mean that?" Tilda questioned.

"I think really," Rudolph went on, "I must have fallen in love with you when we were driving away from Munich in the Police wagon and you were so brave, so calm and un-hysterical."

He laughed.

"We might have been taking a drive in the Park. I knew then that I admired you and I thought you looked in the moonlight like a mountain nymph and a part of my dreams,"

"I have never seen anyone as handsome as you," Tilda said, "so I fell in love with you from the first moment I saw you."

That was the truth she thought.

She had fallen in love when she saw him amongst the trees at the *Linderhof* and had watched him kissing Mitzi.

She had not realised that it was love. She only knew that his face, his voice and everything about him made her feel as she had never felt before.

It had been love and she had not recognised it.

Rudolph's arms tightened.

"What will happen to us, darling, if we cannot have each other?" he asked.

"We must! We must be – together!"

Even as Tilda spoke she thought of the Queen, her mother and Prince Maximilian and knew that none of them was of any consequence beside Rudolph.

"What we have to do," he said slowly as if he was considering every word, "Is to try to get married before anyone can stop us."

"But you said my parents could make me – return to them by – law," Tilda said in a frightened voice.

"They could," Rudolph replied, "but they would be unlikely to do so once we were husband and wife. What would be fatal would be to tell them of our intentions until matters have gone too far for them to interfere."

"Yes, of course," Tilda said, "and one thing they would wish to avoid would be a scandal."

Even as she spoke, she realised what a very big scandal it was going to be anyhow, but told herself that she did not care.

"I am trying to think how we can act for the best," Rudolph said.

As he spoke, they heard the outside door opening and they both stiffened.

"Who could it be?" Tilda asked in a frightened whisper.

Then they heard Frau Sturdel's voice calling,

"It's only me. I've come back for the laudanum bottle."

Tilda disengaged herself from Rudolph's encircling arms and went into the kitchen.

Frau Sturdel was taking the laudanum from the shelf together with some extra towels.

"Has the baby arrived?" Tilda asked.

"Yes," Frau Sturdel replied, "and I was right – I thought I would be. It's a girl!"

"I am glad it is over for your sake," Tilda said. "Is the mother all right?"

"Slightly hysterical," Frau Sturdel answered, "and that is why I need a little laudanum for her, but certainly not the dose your husband took!"

"Frau Sturdel!" Rudolph called from the bedroom. "May I speak to you for a moment?"

"But of course," Frau Sturdel answered.

She put the things she had collected down onto the table and said to Tilda,

"Would you like to be very kind, Frau Weber, and make me a cup of coffee?"

"Would you like anything to eat?" Tilda asked, "I could cook you something?"

"I would not say no to a couple of poached eggs," Frau Sturdel answered. "I've been run off my feet with not a moment to myself since I left here and that's a fact!"

"Then I will cook some eggs for you," Tilda said.

She busied herself with the pans wondering as she did so, what Rudolph wanted to say to Frau Sturdel.

They talked together all the time she was preparing the eggs and coffee.

When finally it was ready and she called to Frau Sturdel, she came out of the bedroom in a hurry and ate quickly without talking.

"I must get back," she said gulping down the coffee. "Thank you, Frau Weber, you've put new life into me and that's another fact!"

She set down her cup.

"I'll do what you asked me, Herr Weber," she called to Rudolph, "but I doubt if the carrier can be here before two o'clock."

"That will suit me well," Rudolph called back, "and thank you again!"

Frau Sturdel hurried down the hill and Tilda went back into the bedroom.

"What have you arranged?" she asked.

"Come here!" Rudolph said.

~145~

She walked towards him, her eyes on his. As she sat down beside him, he took her hands and said in a serious tone she had not heard him use before,

"Do you trust me, my darling?"

"You know I do," Tilda answered.

"Then I want you to agree to the plans I have made," he said. "It's not going to be easy for you, but I promise you I am doing what is best for both of us."

"You are – going to – leave me?" Tilda asked perceptively.

"Only for two – perhaps three days," he answered. "There are a great many things to arrange before we can be together, but I promise you that we will be with each other and nothing shall stop us."

"That is – all I want to – hear," Tilda whispered.

He raised her hand to his lips and kissed it passionately.

"I love you!" he said, "I love you so overwhelmingly, so completely that it is difficult to find words to make you understand that nothing, and I mean this, Tilda, nothing, not even God, shall prevent you from being my wife!"

Chapter Seven

The carriage reached the outskirts of Munich and Tilda, peering from the window, said to Frau Sturdel,

"Everything seems quiet enough!"

"That's what always happens," Frau Sturdel commented in a tone of disgust. "The students upset everyone, make a thorough nuisance of themselves and then go back to the University as if nothing had happened!"

It seemed to Tilda as if it had all happened too quickly for her to have time to think or consider what they were doing.

Rudolph had told her that he had arranged with Frau Sturdel for the village carrier to take him to Obernia.

"She says she can trust the man and he will not ask too many questions," he told Tilda.

"I cannot come – with you?" Tilda asked wistfully.

"No, darling," he replied, "you must go to Munich to make your peace with your uncle and tell the man you are betrothed to that you cannot marry him."

"I don't want to leave you," Tilda pleaded.

"It will not be for long," Rudolph said reassuringly. "Once I have everything arranged for our marriage I will send for you and then nothing and nobody will ever separate us again."

"You are sure of that?" Tilda asked.

He swept her into his arms and held her very closely against him.

"How can I convince you," he said, "that the only thing I want is you?"

Tilda looked up at him, her blue eyes very bright and excited.

"Make me – believe you," she whispered.

His mouth was on hers and he kissed her until once again she was a part of him and she could think of nothing but the wonder and rapture of his lips.

Then he said,

"I will send for you or come and fetch you and once we are married we can defy the world to separate us."

"Will they – try?" Tilda asked with a little shiver.

"They would fail," he asserted confidently.

He managed to dress himself, although Tilda knew it gave him quite a considerable amount of pain.

Then, as it drew near to two o'clock, he said,

"I am going to walk down the road to where Frau Sturdel has promised that the carrier will be waiting for me."

"What about – me?" Tilda asked, "How shall I get back to Munich?"

"Once I have reached my own country," he said, "I will arrange for a carriage and servants to take you and Frau Sturdel to Munich."

"Frau Sturdel?" Tilda ejaculated in surprise.

"You cannot imagine I would risk your going alone without someone to look after you?" Rudolph said. "Frau Sturdel is a Bavarian and she will deal, I am certain, very competently with any impertinent or aggressive students."

"She has agreed to this idea?" Tilda asked in surprise.

"I explained to her how essential it was to our future happiness."

"You did not tell her we were not married?"

Rudolph smiled.

"No. I told her we were already married, but I had not broken the news to my parents. They would be very upset and that is why I must go alone to Obernia."

Tilda laughed.

"I must commend you – on your imagination!"

Rudolph made a sound suspiciously like a groan.

"I hate lying." he said, "especially where it concerns you. But for our future, I am prepared to do anything, however reprehensible, if it will result in our being married as soon as possible."

Tilda felt distinctly uncomfortable as she thought of the amount of lies she had told him.

What would he say, site thought, when he knew her real name and that she was supposed to marry his Prince?

Then she told herself that whoever she was, Rudolph would still love her.

At the same time it would be wise not to tell him the truth until they were actually married or at least until the plans for her becoming his wife were too far advanced for him to back out.

Even the thought that he might sacrifice his love for his patriotism and his loyalty to his Ruler made her tremble with fear.

'I must marry him! *I must!*' she told herself.

She knew that now she had fallen in love it was impossible, completely and absolutely impossible, for her to make a *mariage de convenance*.

In England it had not seemed so repugnant to marry a man she had never seen or to accept the future that had been planned for her by Queen Victoria and her parents.

But now Rudolph had awakened in her something that she had not even realised existed.

The flame that he aroused when he kissed her, the rapture and ecstasy she felt at his touch made her know that even to contemplate a future without him was to walk into an impenetrable darkness.

Even so Tilda could not understand how love had come upon her so quickly, which permeated not only herself but her whole world.

There was only Rudolph, her love for him and his love for her. Nothing else mattered – nothing else counted.

Rank, wealth, respect or pride. She had swept them all away in her need for him! She felt that her very heart beat because she was near to him and he loved her.

Rudolph's plans to travel to Obernia had gone so smoothly that she felt more confident that the future would sort itself out and she need not be afraid.

He kissed her a passionate goodbye in the small kitchen.

"Be very careful of yourself, my beloved little angel," he said.

"I shall count the minutes until I – see you again."

"It is an agony beyond words to leave you."

"Why could we have not stayed here a few days more – now we love each other?"

Rudolph smiled.

"Do you really think, my precious, I could go on sleeping with a bolster between us?"

"We could have – taken it– away!" Tilda whispered.

He pulled her closer to him.

"Tilda! Tilda! You have no idea what you ask of a man!"

"It is wrong – to suggest – that?"

"No, my sweet, but angels don't understand the frailties of mere humans!"

"I don't – understand."

"I will explain when we are married," Rudolph murmured.

"Then let's get married – quickly," Tilda begged him.

Rudolph kissed her forehead.

"As quickly as it is possible. That I swear."

"You will be very careful? I am frightened you might be – captured by the Police or the Military."

"I will take great care for your sake."

He kissed her until she could not speak or breathe and then, looking incredibly handsome, he walked away down the side of the hill to where the carrier would be waiting for him.

He moved with a limp and it was obvious that he was bearing as lightly as possible upon his injured leg.

The bandage was hidden by his woollen stocking and Tilda thought that anyone looking at him would not suspect for a moment that he was a student wanted by the Police or a soldier sought by the Army.

She had an agonising fear that when he reached Obernia the Lieutenant and a platoon of soldiers would be waiting for him.

*

Now, as she approached Munich, she was beset by terrifying questions.

Supposing after all they had meant to each other she never heard from him again?

Supposing he was incarcerated in an Obernian prison or confined to Barracks so that he could not communicate with her?

Then she told herself that she was just being over-imaginative!

She must be cool and calm as Rudolph expected her to be because she was English.

It had been nearly five o'clock before a knock at the door had brought Frau Sturdel to her feet.

She had returned to the bungalow half an hour earlier to say that her patient was comfortable and was not expecting her to call again before the morning.

She then changed from her working dress into what Tilda guessed was her best gown.

They sat drinking tea until Frau Sturdel opened the door to see a man in private livery outside.

"The carriage is ready, *gnädige frau*," he said, bowing.

"We will come at once," Frau Sturdel replied.

She lent Tilda a woollen shawl to wrap around her shoulders against the faint chill that was already in the air now that the sun had lost its heat.

"Supposing anyone sees us coming down the hill?" Tilda asked apprehensively.

"If they do," Frau Sturdel answered, "they will not be able to ask questions until I return."

She was smiling and Tilda forced herself not to feel nervous but to hurry beside Frau Sturdel down the twisting path that led to the road that went through the village.

At the bottom of the hill there was a closed carriage of the type that the Earl of Forthampton found convenient tor travelling.

There were two men on the box and a footman up behind.

There was nothing gaudy or particularly noticeable about the vehicle nor the four horses drawing it, except that they were of good bloodstock.

But Tilda knew that to possess such *equipage* meant that Rudolph was well-to-do.

It did not matter to her whether he was rich or poor, she would love him just the same, she thought.

Yet she could not help hoping that he would be wealthy enough to assuage in some way her father's anger when he learnt that she had refused the position of Her Royal Highness for that of an ordinary citizen of Obernia.

As they travelled at a fast pace towards Munich, Frau Sturdel piped up,

"I don't mind telling you, Frau Weber, this is a treat for me. It's not often I journey by carriage and it's something I greatly enjoy."

"I am glad," Tilda smiled, "because it is very kind of you to come with me."

"Your husband was worried about you," Frau Sturdel said. "He is very much in love, as I am sure you know! Ah well, you are a lucky couple! There is so much unhappiness in the world today that it is a pleasure to see two people who were really meant for each other."

"Do you really think – that?" Tilda asked gazing at her wide-eyed.

"I am sure of it," Frau Sturdel said, "and it would be difficult to find a more handsome pair. Indeed your husband would have far too many women making eyes at him for your peace of mind, if it was not for the fact that you are so lovely that he has eyes only for you!"

"I hope that is true," Tilda said in a low voice.

She could not help feeling a little jealous of Mitzi and the other women Rudolph had loved before he met her.

He was so overwhelmingly good-looking that she knew it would be impossible for there not to have been women – many, many women in his life.

But he loved her!

There was no doubt about his sincerity or indeed the fact that, while he had been prepared never to see her again, he had suddenly changed his mind.

She could only believe that it was because he said he found it impossible to live without her,

Tilda gave a little sigh.

It was going to be hard to wait for his message and, when the moment came, to tell Lady Crewkerne that she did not intend to marry the Prince.

She could only pray that when she arrived in Munich she would not find a message from His Royal Highness commanding them to leave immediately for Obernia.

She had not dared tell Rudolph that there might be difficulties about her staying on in Munich.

Then she told herself that she would contrive it somehow, even if she had to take to her bed and say that she was ill.

It had been difficult to decide how he should get in touch with her when he believed her name to be 'Hyde'.

But rather than tell him a lot of lies that might make him suspicious, Tilda decided that the only thing to do was to inform the desk at the hotel that any messages for 'Miss Tilda Hyde' were to be given to her immediately.

'They may think it strange,' she told herself, 'but what does it matter?'

Philosophically she shrugged her shoulders. The curiosity of the hotel concierge was of no consequence. What was of great importance at the moment was not to arouse Rudolph's suspicions in any way.

The carriage was now driving through the main streets of Munich.

It was getting dusk and the gaslights were glowing golden in the twilight.

There were many citizens in the streets, but they all appeared to be moving peacefully about their business or taking a stroll towards the cafés where there were crowds sitting at tables on the pavement and drinking beer.

"We shall be at the hotel in a moment," Frau Sturdel remarked.

"I can only thank you again," Tilda said, "I don't believe that anyone in the world could be as kind as you have been to me and to my husband."

"It's been a real pleasure," Frau Sturdel declared, "and to tell the truth it has brought a bit of excitement into my life. I shall often laugh to think how my grandmother's quilt hid you from *Herr Oberpolizei-Inspektor*! I shall also remember this carriage ride. It has been such a treat, it has really!"

"It seems a long way for you to come just to turn about and go back again," Tilda said.

"Don't worry about me," Frau Sturdel insisted. "I'll sit back and pretend I'm a Lady of Quality driving in my own carriage to a Reception with the Mayor!"

Tilda laughed and, as the horses came to a standstill, she bent to kiss Frau Sturdel's cheek.

"As soon as we are settled," she said, "I will write to you and perhaps one day you will come and see us."

"I shall enjoy that more than I can say. Please don't forget to ask me."

"I shall not do that," Tilda said, "and we shall always be grateful, my husband and I."

She kissed the elderly woman again.

But, as she stepped out of the carriage, she suddenly felt very small and afraid of what lay ahead.

Then instinctively her chin went up.

What did it matter what anybody said?

Rudolph was waiting for her! Rudolph was going to marry her!

Rudolph loved her!

She passed through the vestibule and went up to the first floor in a slow creaky lift.

She thought that the liftman looked at her curiously, but he did not speak and, reaching the first floor, she walked to the sitting room that was part of their suite.

Taking a deep breath she opened the door.

There were three people sitting on the heavy brocade furniture.

They all turned their heads to stare at her with something like stupefaction.

The Professor spoke first,

"Lady Victoria!"

"I am sorry if you have been waiting for me – " Tilda began.

Then she recognised the third person present.

He was a young man who had changed very little even though it was seven years since she last saw him.

*

Francis Tetherton was her cousin and was an attaché in the British Embassy in Obernia.

"You will see Francis when you reach Obernia," her mother had said to her. "I know you always found him a bore, Tilda, but you must be nice to him and ask him to the Palace from time to time."

But now Tilda had a very different idea about Francis.

She walked across the room with her hands outstretched.

"Oh, Cousin Francis, I am so pleased to see you!" she exclaimed.

Effete, pompous and rather stupid, Francis Tetherton replied,

"Cousin Victoria, we have been so worried about you!"

"Very worried indeed," Lady Crewkerne said sharply. "Where have you been, Lady Victoria, and why did you not communicate with us? After the disgraceful and reprehensible manner in which you and the Professor behaved, as you might have imagined, I have been extremely anxious."

Tilda glanced at the Professor.

She could see that he had been browbeaten by Lady Crewkerne and had a 'hangdog' apologetic look about him, which made her feel sorry for him.

"I expect the Professor has told you," she replied, "that everything was my fault."

"There are two opinions on that!" Lady Crewkerne said acidly. "How any man could dare to take you in your position to such a – "

"Wait a minute!" Tilda said. "Let's get this straight. The Professor did not take me – he accompanied me when he knew that I was determined to go to the Beer Hall alone – yes alone – by myself!"

She saw that her words and the manner in which she spoke surprised Lady Crewkerne and she went on,

"What is more, I do *not* suppose the Professor has told you how it was entirely due to his bravery that I was saved from being trampled underfoot by students or, worse still, shot by them! He saved my life and I shall always be grateful to him."

"The Professor did not tell us that," Lady Crewkerne said in a somewhat mollified tone of voice.

"It sounds as if the Professor acted bravely in very difficult circumstances," Francis Tetherton said with a slow pomposity that had always irritated Tilda.

However she had a good reason for being pleasant to him and she flattered him with her attention while raising his and Lady Crewkerne's estimation of the Professor until he no longer appeared so hangdog.

She also invented a long and rather garbled account of how, swept away by the students to a poor part of the City, she had finally taken refuge at a house of a kind midwife.

There had been continuous rioting outside and it was not until this evening that the midwife had been able to bring her back to the hotel.

It all sounded plausible and anyway there was nothing Lady Crewkerne and the others could do but accept her version of what had happened.

When Tilda had finished her tale, Lady Crewkerne said,

"Now I am sure, Lady Victoria, you would like a bath and rid yourself of that strange fancy dress you are garbed in."

"I would indeed," Tilda replied. "But will you excuse me, ma'am, if I first have a private word with my cousin? There is something I want to ask him."

"Of course. Lady Victoria," Lady Crewkerne said. "I will go and see that Hannah has everything ready for you in your bedroom."

She and the Professor left the sitting room and Tilda turned to her cousin.

"I want you to do something for me, Cousin Francis."

"What is it?" he enquired.

"Before I tell you," Tilda replied, "I have not yet asked you why you are here."

She thought his eyes shifted nervously.

"The Ambassador thought that I should reassure you," he said, "that the arrangements are going ahead for your reception into Obernia."

"And yet there is still some delay?" Tilda asked.

"Unfortunately, yes," Francis Tetherton replied.

"And whose fault is that?"

There was a perceptible pause before Francis Tetherton answered,

"His Royal Highness does not wish you to arrive until everything is planned to his satisfaction."

"He knows I am here?"

"Our Ambassador has been in communication with the Prime Minister and the Cabinet," Francis Tetherton answered. "We realise in a way that the delay is somewhat of a slight, but there is really nothing we can do without the approval of His Royal Highness."

"That makes it easier for you to take him my request," Tilda said slowly.

"What request?" Francis Tetherton asked.

"I want – no – I *insist*, on seeing the Prince before I enter Obernia."

Francis Tetherton looked at Tilda in consternation.

"But that is impossible! It is being arranged, Cousin Victoria, for you to meet His Royal Highness formally on the steps of the Palace."

Tilda said nothing and he went on,

"The Prime Minister, the Foreign Secretary and the British Ambassador will receive you at the border. Then you will drive in State to the Capital where Prince Maximilian will be waiting."

Tilda took a deep breath.

"I do not intend to agree to any of that, Cousin Francis, unless the Prince sees me alone. Either here or somewhere else suitable."

"I really don't understand," Francis Tetherton moaned.

"It's quite simple," Tilda replied. "I wish to meet him unofficially and talk with him. It has to be before I enter Obernia."

"It is impossible! Quite impossible!" Francis Tetherton exclaimed positively.

"In which case the Prime Minister, the Foreign Secretary and the British Ambassador will have to wait indefinitely," Tilda said.

"Cousin Victoria, you cannot be saying these things!"

"But I *am* saying them!"

"But the Prince is Royal! He is Head of the State. You cannot order him to come and see you as if he was a private individual."

"He is still my prospective husband," Tilda answered "and, as his prospective wife, I presume I have certain privileges? Anyway I intend to see him alone and it is up to you to arrange it!"

"I cannot! You must see that it is not the sort of thing that I or even the Ambassador can do. If you want to talk with His Royal Highness, you can do so after your arrival."

"You will kindly make it clear that there will be no arrival, no State drive, unless I have seen the Prince beforehand."

"It is the most absurd request I have ever heard," Francis Tetherton said crossly.

Tilda gave a little yawn.

"I am really very tired, Cousin Francis," she said, "and so I think I will go to bed. I expect you will be staying for dinner, but this is not something we can discuss in front of Lady Crewkerne or the Professor."

"You don't wish them to know of your crazy idea?" Francis Tetherton asked rudely.

"I think it would be very mistaken of you to tell them," Tilda smiled, "for nothing and no one will alter my determination in any way. I intend to see Prince Maximilian. If you will not tell him so, I will find somebody who will."

"It is impossible – absolutely impossible!" Francis Tetherton repeated again.

"In which case you can tell the Prince that I am returning to England."

"I cannot believe I am hearing you correctly," her cousin groaned. "This is not the way a well-brought-up young English girl should behave."

Tilda laughed.

"If you are casting aspersions on Papa and Mama for the way they have raised me, Cousin Francis, it is something I do not think they will appreciate."

"I imagine that neither your father nor your mother would condone your behaviour at the moment," Francis Tetherton retorted. "You don't understand, Cousin Victoria, it has been enough worry that you have been missing the past three days."

"Fortunately there is no reason for the Prince to learn of that."

"No, but to ask him to see you alone – it is not protocol, it is not etiquette, it is *not* the done thing."

"I am not prepared to argue. Cousin Francis," Tilda said. "If you will explain to the Prince that I have something of great importance to say to him and that I will not enter his country until I have said it, he will see me."

She paused a moment to add,

"After all, he owes me something for having kept me waiting all this time in Munich."

"You were not here, so he was not really keeping you waiting," Francis Tetherton said rather feebly.

"Are you prepared to explain that to His Royal Highness?" Tilda asked.

She walked towards the door.

"I am not going to stand here arguing, Cousin Francis. Tell the Prince that whatever the arrangements he has made in Obernia, I shall be unavoidably detained in Munich until we have met."

The consternation on Francis Tetherton's face was laughable, but Tilda's expression was one of elation.

She went into her bedroom where Hannah, very disagreeable and extremely critical, was waiting for her.

*

The following day Tilda went sightseeing.

The Professor and a slightly mollified Lady Crewkerne accompanied her.

At the same time there was a distinct coldness between her two chaperones, which Tilda chose to ignore.

She had wanted to see Munich and the Professor's spirits rose as they went from museum to museum, to the *Pinakothek* with its wonderful pictures and the *Marienplatz* to stare at the *glockenspiel*.

They visited Churches where Tilda looked for a long time at the profusion of carved angels.

She was thrilled that Rudolph had compared her to the small joyous creatures that seemed to express a happiness that was beyond the reach of mere humans.

'I will make Rudolph happy!' Tilda vowed to herself. 'I will bring him a joy that no other woman has been able to give him.'

Sometimes when she thought of Mitzi's red lips and pretty provocative face she felt that she might fail him.

It was the following morning that Francis Tetherton reappeared.

As soon as she saw him, Tilda knew that he had something to tell her.

She took him alone into the sitting room so that she could hear the news.

"The Prince will see me?" she asked impatiently, unable to wait for Francis's slow pronouncement.

"His Royal Highness will see you this evening," Francis Tetherton answered, "but I don't mind telling you, Cousin Victoria, it was very difficult to persuade him. He kept asking me what you had to say. Of course I had no idea."

"But he will see me. Will he come here?"

"No, it is too far," Francis Tetherton answered, "but I will take you to an inn that is on the border of Obernia and Bavaria."

"*The Royal Boundary*," Tilda exclaimed.

Her cousin looked at her in surprise.

"That is right!" he answered. "How did you hear of it?"

Tilda thought of the Lieutenant who was hoping to dine with her there and smiled secretly.

Aloud she said,

"What time are we to meet His Royal Highness?"

"At nine-thirty and, if you don't want Lady Crewkerne to ask questions, I had better say I am taking you to a Reception given by some friends of mine."

"She will be affronted that she has not been invited, but who cares? It was clever of you to arrange what I wanted, Cousin Francis, and thank you very much."

"I just hope you realise. Cousin Victoria, what a tremendous concession His Royal Highness is making in granting a request of this sort. I only hope you will show your appreciation suitably at being accorded such a privilege."

Knowing that she intended to tell the Prince that she had no wish to marry him. Tilda thought expressions of humble gratitude were hardly suitable.

But she said nothing and passed the rest of the day planning what she should say to the Prince.

She told herself that as Rudolph was Obernian she would have to be very careful not to bring down upon him the displeasure of his Ruler, perhaps to the point where Prince Maximilian would seek his revenge.

The idea that Rudolph might be banished, imprisoned or persecuted in some way was terrifying.

Then she told herself that the Prince would be big-minded enough to accept that in this day and age one could not force a woman to the altar if she was determined to say 'no'.

Equally all her fears came rushing back into her mind – the whispered innuendos, the half sentences that had been started and stopped when people found she was listening.

Why had Prince Maximilian incurred the disapproval of her relatives? And strangest of all why had he refused ever to be painted or photographed?

Perhaps, she told herself, he had had an accident out riding and his face was now repulsive.

Perhaps there were reasons beyond her comprehension that made decent people find him almost repellent.

Whatever the mystery about Prince Maximilian it would not concern her now. She was not going to marry him and once they had talked tonight, there was no reason for them ever to meet again.

Nevertheless as time passed Tilda knew that the calmness and coolness that Rudolph had admired for her were rapidly giving way to agitation.

Suppose the Prince categorically refused to break their engagement?

Supposing he informed her that he would not even listen to her and merely answered that the plans for their wedding would go ahead?

Suppose – even more frightening – he ensured that Rudolph could not marry her because he was not free to do so.

It was the thought of this that made Tilda decide that whatever happened she would not let the Prince know who Rudolph was.

She would simply tell him that she could not marry him because she was in love with somebody else.

Wild horses would not drag Rudolph's name to her lips if she thought that it might damage him.

It suddenly struck her that in the circumstances they might not be allowed to live in Obernia.

Perhaps they would have to move to Bavaria or Austria.

Now for the first time she realised how little she knew about Rudolph.

He was a soldier, but a rather reprehensible one. That fact was established,

But who and what were his parents?

To be in a Cavalry Regiment usually meant one was of Social consequence.

Tilda remembered her father saying that in the German Cavalry Regiments thirty-four of the Officers were Princes and fifty-one were Counts.

It might be different in Obernia, although she doubted it, and the Lieutenant had seemed blue-blooded.

There had never seemed time to talk to Rudolph of anything except themselves, but now she realised that there were many things she should have asked him before they separated.

Then she told herself that Rudolph was a gentleman because to her he had always been kind and understanding.

He had never shocked or frightened or even embarrassed her as he might easily have done, considering that they had been shut up together in one room and she had even slept in the same bed beside him.

For the first time, innocent though she was, she vaguely understood there might have been hidden dangers and terrors in such a situation although she had no conception of what they might be.

Rudolph had said to her,

"*You must not drive me too hard, Tilda. I am a man but I am trying to behave decently, as you would expect of a gentleman.*"

He had behaved decently, but she was not quite certain what would have happened had he behaved indecently.

It had been impossible not to trust him, although she had driven him 'too hard' so that he had kissed her when he had not meant to and he had asked her to be his wife.

'He must not be hurt by our marriage,' Tilda said to herself. 'I must be clever with the Prince so that he is not angry or vindictive.'

Nevertheless, as she drove away from Munich beside Francis Tetherton, she was too tense and too apprehensive to have much to say.

Francis was also nervous. She knew that by the way he kept fidgeting with his tie and dragging his gold watch from his waistcoat pocket to look at the time.

He had hurried her from the hotel after they had eaten a light dinner and they therefore arrived at *The Royal Boundary* too early.

"I have engaged a private room," Francis Tetherton said, "so walk quickly through the vestibule. We don't want anyone to see you. They will think it very strange for you to be here alone with a man."

"No one is likely to recognise me," Tilda remarked.

Despite Francis's protests she could not refrain from peeping into the restaurant to see where she might have dined with the Lieutenant.

It was a very attractive room with oak beams, stuffed heads of wild animals on the walls and small tables lit with candles.

There were a number of people having dinner and Francis Tetherton pulled her down a passage and into a small oak-panelled parlour where a log fire was burning.

Francis Tetherton looked at his watch for the hundredth time.

"You stay here, Cousin Victoria," he said. "I will go and wait for His Royal Highness at the entrance. He will certainly not wish to be recognised and I will bring him here immediately upon his arrival."

He spoke in an agitated tone and Tilda wondered why Rudolph had the impression that the English were always cool and calm.

"I will be all right, Cousin Francis," she answered, "you go and look for His Royal Highness."

Francis Tetherton went away and Tilda walked somewhat restlessly backwards and forwards across the room.

She was rehearsing yet again in her mind exactly what she would say to the Prince.

She was confident that eventually she would get her own way and he would free her from the engagement that was not of her choosing and, she suspected, not of his either.

It was, she was certain, entirely due to Queen Victoria that Prince Maximilian had been persuaded in the first place to have an English wife.

'There are doubtless many Princesses in Austria and Bavaria he would have preferred,' Tilda told herself. 'At the same time, because they are all so frightened of England and more especially of Queen Victoria, he has had to agree. Perhaps he will even be glad to be rid of me.'

She could not help knowing that not only Prince Maximilian would be worried as to what Queen Victoria would say, but her mother, who was frightened of Her Majesty, would feel humiliated by her behaviour.

'Poor Mama,' Tilda thought to herself, 'but I am sure that when she meets Rudolph she will love him.'

The very thought of Rudolph brought a warm glow to her heart.

She felt a little thrill run through her as she thought of how closely he had held her in his arms and how passionately he had kissed her.

Why should she care about a Royal position, she asked herself, or the approval of her stuffy relatives when she could be loved as Rudolph loved her?

'I am not afraid of the Prince,' Tilda told herself, 'I am not afraid of anything except of losing Rudolph.'

She could hear again the note in his voice as he said,

"*Nothing, not even God, shall prevent you from being my wife.*"

And nothing would prevent him from being her husband, Tilda vowed.

At that moment the door opened.

She drew in her breath!

She turned to see not, as she had anticipated, a strange man who she expected would be Prince Maximilian, but *Rudolph*!

Advancing into the room, Rudolph looked for the moment incredulous when he saw her.

Before Tilda could speak he exclaimed,

"Tilda, my precious darling! What are you doing here?"

She ran towards him feeling that it could not be true.

She could touch him.

She could lift her face to his.

For a moment he looked down into her eyes and then his lips were on hers.

She could feel again the wonder and rapture she had longed for as he kissed passionately and demandingly until she felt as if her body melted into his.

After what seemed a century of ecstasy, Rudolph raised his head.

"I have missed you!" he said hoarsely, "Oh, God, how I have missed you!"

"Do you still – love me?" Tilda asked.

"You know I do."

Then, with an effort as if he forced himself to think sensibly he asked,

"But why are you here?"

"I am meeting the – man to whom I am – betrothed," Tilda replied.

"To tell him you cannot marry him? My darling, then you will be free!"

"I will be free," Tilda repeated, "when can I – come to – you?"

"Perhaps tomorrow," he said, "but certainly the next day. I cannot wait any longer."

"Neither can – I," Tilda whispered.

His lips were on hers again and it was impossible to speak, only to feel.

Then abruptly he took his arms from her and said,

"If you are meeting this man you are engaged to, I had better leave you alone."

"Why are you here?" Tilda asked.

He was about to answer her when the door opened and Francis Tetherton looked into the room.

"Are you all right, Cousin Victoria?" he enquired.

Then he saw Rudolph, straightened himself and bowed his head.

"I am sorry, Sire," he said. "I did not know you had arrived. I must have been waiting at the wrong entrance."

There was no answer from either Tilda or Rudolph, who was staring at him as if transfixed and he added,

"I will see that you are not disturbed, Sire."

He disappeared, shutting the door behind him.

For the moment there was a paralysed silence and then Rudolph said in a voice Tilda did not recognise,

"He called you 'Victoria'. What is your name?"

Tilda's eyes were on his face.

For a moment it was impossible to answer him.

Again Rudolph asked insistently,

"I asked you *what* is your name?"

It seemed to Tilda as if someone else answered for her.

"Victoria – Matilda Tetherton-Smythe," she said hardly above a whisper.

Then, as Rudolph stared at her apparently speechless, she added,

"Why did Cousin Francis call you 'Sire'? And why was he waiting for – you?"

Rudolph took a step forward.

"Are you telling me the truth?" he asked. "Is that *really* your name?"

He spoke fiercely and then suddenly he began to laugh.

He walked across the room to lean on the mantelpiece.

"It cannot, be true!" he laughed. "It cannot be true!"

"What cannot? What are you – saying? Why are you – laughing?" Tilda asked.

She did not understand.

Something strange and frightening had happened.

For a moment she felt very lost and very alone.

Rudolph looked at her and his laughter died away.

As if realising her uncertainty, her fear, he held out his arms and she ran towards him.

"It's all right, my darling," he said, "everything is all right! But I have given my Prime Minister a heart attack because I told him that, unless I can marry a girl called Tilda Hyde, I will abdicate!"

Chapter Eight

The tree-lined streets were filled with crowds cheering, waving flags and throwing flowers into the open carriage.

There were houses decorated with garlands and arches with the words, *Welcome to Obernia* and *God Bless Victoria*, written on them.

It was all very exciting and Tilda's eyes were alight as she waved to the happy smiling people.

She looked entrancing in a gown the colour of her eyes and a bonnet trimmed with small pink rosebuds. She carried a tiny blue sunshade also decorated with rosebuds.

Beside her in the carriage sat the Prime Minister of Obernia, still handsome despite his years and opposite him, the white plumes of his hat floating in the breeze, was the British Ambassador. Beside him was the Obernian Foreign Secretary.

They had met Tilda at the border.

She had been obliged to listen to a lengthy and somewhat boring address of welcome and it was difficult not to show her impatience when she was counting the minutes until she could see Rudolph again.

It still seemed incredible that Rudolph should be Prince Maximilian, the man she had been determined not to marry, the man she had expected to feel a repugnance for.

"How can you be the Prince?" she had exclaimed incredulously, "I thought you were – deformed!"

"Deformed?" Rudolph repeated in astonishment.

"Everybody was so mysterious about you," Tilda explained, "they were always whispering and then lapsing into an embarrassed silence whenever I entered the room.

Besides there were no pictures of you and I was told that you refused to be photographed."

Rudolph hesitated before replying and she fancied that he looked embarrassed.

"I think I now understand why you were so secretive!" Tilda cried. "It is because you wanted to escape from time to time and you were afraid people would recognise you!"

Rudolph smiled.

"You are too perceptive!" he said, "but yes, it's true, I did sometimes play truant."

"Absent without leave!"

"How could I imagine those bungling idiots would send a search party for me? But that, of course, was your fault!"

"*My* fault?" Tilda asked.

"No – it was really mine," Rudolph conceded. "My Comptroller told me that you might be delayed on such a long journey so I went off into the blue without saying where I was going!"

He smiled.

"When the Palace learnt that you had arrived exactly on time, they panicked. It had been arranged for you to come to Obernia a week before the wedding so that we could get to know each other."

"That was just what we were doing!" Tilda exclaimed.

"Fortunately the Royal Household were unaware of that!" Rudolph smiled.

Tilda laughed.

"You must have upset them a great deal one way and another?"

"They were always fussing over me like a bunch of clucking hens, disapproving and criticising," Rudolph said.

"That is why I called myself by my second name and, when I could stand no more of it, I disappeared."

"Where did you go?"

"To find new friends."

"Who were, of course, pretty ladies?"

"None of them as lovely as you."

"But – you – loved them! "

Rudolph did not answer for a moment and then he said,

"There are different sorts of love, my precious."

"Explain – to – me."

He chose his words carefully.

"Most women are like lovely flowers. A man wants to pick them, but usually they fade quickly."

Tilda was listening intently as he went on,

"But, even though he tells himself that he is only seeking amusement, he will hope that each flower will be different and that one will be the perfect and exceptional blossom he has always longed to find."

"And – when – he does – find it?"

"Then it is his forever and it brings him real and true happiness."

"And he no longer – goes on – seeking?" Tilda asked.

"No, all that is finished."

"Are you sure?" she asked. "I should be – miserable if you vanished and I had no idea where you had gone."

"I swear to you I did not look when I promised you I would not do so," Rudolph said, "but St. Gerhardt's penalty has nevertheless come true. There will be only one woman in my life until I die!"

"Are you sure?" Tilda asked.

"So sure," he answered, "that every painter and photographer in Europe can attend our wedding for all I care!"

He drew her very close as he said,

"Besides, my darling, I want pictures of you to show the world how unbelievably beautiful you are."

Then he was kissing her again and nothing else was of any consequence.

*

The Capital of Obernia lay in a fertile valley with snow-peaked mountains rising high on either side of it and, when Tilda saw the Palace, it was just as she had imagined it would be.

There was a long wide road lined with cheering crowds that led up to the huge gold-tipped wrought-iron gates.

Beyond them was a gleaming white building with pillars and colonnades, arched doorways and exquisite statues silhouetted against the skyline.

"It's so lovely!" Tilda exclaimed out loud.

The Prime Minister looked at her appreciatively.

He had told her that His Royal Highness had insisted that their wedding should take place late this afternoon.

Tilda had known that not only was the Prime Minister apprehensive in case she should consider such a ceremony on the day of her arrival over-precipitate, but so was the Ambassador.

"That will be wonderful!'" she had exclaimed and saw their surprise at her enthusiasm.

'I must be careful!' she told herself. 'They none of them must guess that I have already met Rudolph.'

Francis Tetherton had been sworn to secrecy, but she wondered what the Prime Minister had thought when the Prince had made such a rapid change of heart.

He must have thought it extraordinary when Rudolph returned to Obernia to say that, after all his talk of abdication, he was prepared to marry Lady Victoria Tetherton-Smythe at once.

"Are you going to explain why?" Tilda had asked.

"I think explanations would involve us in too many implications," he answered with a gentle smile.

He put his fingers under her chin and lifted her face up to his as he said,

"How could you have been so naughty as to go to a Beer Hall? Heaven knows what trouble you might have found yourself in."

"I was in trouble, but only with – you."

"We can thank God for that!" Rudolph said in a solemn voice.

"I cannot think what Mama would say if she knew that we had spent three nights together at Frau Sturdel's house," Tilda teased, "and even slept in the same bed!"

"We can only hope that she will never hear of it and do remember, my sweet love, to behave formally and perhaps a little shyly when we meet each other at the Palace."

"I will try!" Tilda murmured.

"God knows it will not be easy for me to keep my hands off you."

"I hope you will think I look pretty," Tilda told him. "I have a special gown to arrive in and you have only ever seen me in a peasant costume."

"In which you looked like an angel – a very alluring little angel!"

"You made that an excuse not to – kiss me." Tilda said resentfully.

"I tried to behave with propriety and I failed."

"I am – glad."

"A man would have to be blind or a Saint not to be tempted by your lips."

"I want to – tempt– you."

"And I hope never again to go through the agony of sleeping next to you with a bolster between us."

"You put – it – there!" Tilda said,

"I know – it was the only solution – otherwise I could not have prevented myself from touching you."

"I would have – liked that." Tilda whispered.

*

As the horses swept round the huge fountain that was playing in front of the long flight of steps that led up to the ornate Palace doors, Tilda saw Rudolph waiting for her.

She forgot his warnings, his instructions and everything but her joy at seeing him.

He was looking magnificent in a white Regimental tunic with gold epaulettes, a profusion of decorations and a blue ribbon across his chest.

The horses came to a standstill.

It was difficult to wait with suitable composure as the footmen opened the door, let down the steps and removed the light rug that had covered Tilda's gown.

The ground was bestrewn with flowers that had been thrown by the crowds and Tilda looked like a spring nymph as she stepped out from amongst a cloud of blossom.

"There are six steps to walk up," the Ambassador had told her, "and His Royal Highness will come down six steps so that you meet halfway."

"I am sure that everything has been very carefully planned. Your Excellency," Tilda said demurely.

"I can only hope that it all goes smoothly," the Ambassador said in a worried voice. "We have had some difficulty in getting His Royal Highness to agree to our suggestions until the very last moment."

Tilda smiled secretly to herself.

She wondered what the Ambassador would think if he knew that until the very last moment His Royal Highness had decided not to marry the English bride who had been chosen for him by Queen Victoria.

It was still hard to credit that Rudolph had really been so obstinately determined to marry no one except an unknown girl called Tilda Hyde that he had threatened to abdicate.

"Do you really love me?" Tilda asked him before they had parted in *The Royal Boundary*.

"I will prove that very clearly," he answered, "as soon as we are married and you really are my wife."

"That is what I want to be," Tilda whispered.

"And that is what you are going to be, my adorable one," he answered.

Once again before he left he warned her that their adventures must remain a complete secret.

"No one would be surprised at anything I am said to have done and they would make up most of the scandal anyway," he said. "But you are different. They will expect you to be very circumspect."

"I will try to be pompous and stuffy like our relatives!"

Now, as Tilda walked up the steps towards Rudolph, she knew it was impossible to hide the gladness in her eyes or prevent little thrills running through her because once again she was near him.

She had never imagined that even he could look so incredibly handsome nor so commanding and authoritative.

She reached the sixth step and he put out his hand to take hers.

"May I have the great privilege and honour of welcoming your Ladyship to Obernia?" he asked. "This is a very auspicious day for my country and a moment of great joy to me personally."

After he had spoken, he raised her hand to his lips and she felt his fingers tighten on hers.

He raised his head and, as Tilda looked up into his eyes, for a moment it was impossible to speak or remember the speech that she had rehearsed so carefully.

'I love you!' she wanted to shout out.

Then with difficulty and stumbling a little over the words, she said,

"I am deeply grateful for Your Royal Highness's words of welcome. It is an inexpressible pleasure to be here in Obernia and know that this beautiful country will be my future home."

The words were said.

Then, beneath her breath in a whisper that was audible only to Rudolph, Tilda whispered,

"You look so handsome, so magnificent! I want to – kiss you!"

She saw the answer in his eyes and knew that it was an effort for him to offer her his arm conventionally.

"Allow me to escort your Ladyship into the Palace," he proclaimed formally.

She took his arm and they went up the steps together followed by the Prime Minister and the Ambassador. The other officials waiting on the steps moved into line behind them.

"Where are we going?" Tilda asked.

"You will be introduced to Members of the Government and the Court officials," Rudolph answered, "and then you will retire to change into your wedding gown."

"I want to be – alone with you," Tilda said softly.

"I want it too" Rudolph replied, "but it will be impossible until after we are married."

"Do you not want to – kiss me?"

"You know I do," he answered and she heard the deep note of desire in his voice, "but we must behave properly, my dearest heart."

"Why?" she asked. "What is the point of being a Royal Prince if you cannot do as you like?"

Her words had been spoken *sotto voce* and now Rudolph said loudly,

"I hope your Ladyship will admire the pictures in this part of the Palace. Many of them, of course, depict our joint ancestors – Kings, Queens and Rulers of neighbouring States."

"I must be – alone with you! *I must*! If only for a moment," Tilda murmured. "It is going to be hours and hours until we are married and I have – missed you."

"I have missed you too." Rudolph replied, "But we have to be careful."

"You are over cautious!" Tilda teased. "Almost – cowardly."

~180~

"This is a fine portrait of Frederick the Great," Rudolph announced. "I think you will agree that the artist did him justice."

"It is very fine!" Tilda agreed.

Then beneath her breath,

"Shall I – pretend to faint? Then at least you would have to – pick me up in your – arms!"

"Tilda, my precious, do behave. You are such a naughty angel!"

"I promise I will be very good if I can kiss you – just once."

He paused to show her another picture and then he said out of the side of his mouth,

"We turn a corner in a moment. There is a door on the right where my father's decorations are displayed. We could slip into it quickly!"

"I knew you would see sense!" Tilda muttered with elation.

"There is nothing sensible about it!" Rudolph groaned.

They turned the corner with the long procession still behind them.

Rudolph pulled Tilda through a door on the right hand side, closed it behind them and locked it.

She gave a cry of sheer happiness.

Then she was in his arms and he was kissing her wildly and passionately as if they had passed through unknown dangers to find each other.

"I love you! *I adore you*!" Rudolph murmured, "but this is crazy."

"Delicious – heavenly – craziness!" she replied.

It was difficult to move or breathe as he almost lifted her off her feet.

Then the handle of the door was being turned and the Prime Minister's voice asked,

"Is there anything wrong, Your Royal Highness?"

Rudolph released Tilda and she saw the fire in his eyes as he said,

"I want you! Dear God, *how I want you*!"

He saw Tilda's face light up as if there were a thousand candles burning inside her.

"That is what I – longed for you to say more than – anything else."

With a superhuman effort Rudolph turned the key in the lock and opened the door at the same moment.

"There seems to be something wrong with this catch," he said in a matter of fact tone. "I was just showing Lady Victoria my father's decorations."

"They are – thrilling!" Tilda said in a soft voice.

*

Driving back from the Cathedral the Archduke Ferdinand Holstein Mittlegratz sat back in the open carriage with a rattle of his sword and said,

"That poor sweet innocent child! I will murder young Maximilian with my own hands if he does not behave properly towards her!"

The Archduchess glanced at him with a half-smile on her lips.

"You know, Ferdinand," she said, "I have a feeling that our Romeo Prince will no longer go a-roaming."

"I don't know why you should think that," the Archduke growled. "He has chased every pretty woman from here to Finland for long enough! I will not have him upsetting that sweet, gentle little creature who is hardly out of the nursery and I am quite prepared to tell him so in no uncertain terms!"

"And if Maximilian does go on causing scandals, which I suspect were over-exaggerated anyway, what can you do about it?" the Archduchess asked.

"I will myself protect Victoria!" the Archduke replied with fervour.

His wife laughed.

"I am sure you will, Ferdinand, that is if you can get anywhere near her."

"What do you mean by that?" the Archduke enquired.

"I mean," his wife replied, "that, when we were in the Cathedra, I watched the sentimental manner in which you were yearning protectively over the bride and what I saw in your face was echoed in the eyes of nearly every man present."

"Well, what about it?"

"I cannot help thinking," the Archduchess went on, "that Maximilian will be far too busy looking after his wife in the future to have time for his own philandering."

"Let us hope you are right," the Archduke snorted.

"What is more," the Archduchess continued, "I think little Victoria has more idea of how to look after herself than you give her credit for."

"She is simple, unsophisticated, innocent of the world and nothing more than a baby!" the Archduke retorted.

He spoke quite ferociously and his wife with a side-glance at him replied meekly,

"I am sure you know best, Ferdinand!"

But at the same time her eyes were twinkling.

*

The fire had burnt low, but still gave enough light to show the outline of the great bed with its carved canopy of gold angels and its hangings of pink velvet, which made it appear like an over-blown rose.

There were two heads very close together on the pillows edged with lace and embroidered with the Royal crown.

Rudolph reached out to pull Tilda closer to him. She was soft and yielding as she said,

"Rudolph, I want to ask you – something."

"What is it, my precious, my perfect little love?"

As he spoke, he gently swept her fair hair back from her forehead so that he could kiss it.

"I was just – wondering," Tilda whispered, "when you will do the 'unpleasant things' Mama talked about."

Rudolph drew her a little closer.

"I believe, my darling, your Mama was referring to what we have already done."

Tilda gave a little exclamation and turned her face up to his.

"You think that Mama was talking about – making love?" she asked. "But it was wonderful – marvellous – the most perfect thing I could ever – imagine!"

"Do you mean that?" Rudolph asked in his deep voice.

"You know I mean it," Tilda answered. "I did not know I could be so – happy or that I could feel so – wildly – excited."

"Do I really excite you?"

"So very – very – much!"

"My darling, I worship you!"

"We – belong to each – other."

"For ever!" Rudolph vowed.

"All I want is to be with you," Tilda said, "and for you to – make love to me and – kiss me – all the time."

"That is what I want too, but we shall also have some official duties."

"I don't mind as long as we do them together."

"We will always be together, but you must be good, my sweet."

"I will – very – very good!" Tilda promised him.

"It was not very good in the middle of the ceremony in the Cathedral to ask me if Mitzi was present," Rudolph admonished her. "I am sure the Archbishop heard you."

"I just wondered if you had invited her."

"No, of course I did not!" Rudolph answered, "and you should not even have heard of someone like Mitzi."

"You should be grateful to her," Tilda answered. "It was when I saw you kissing her that I fell in love with you."

"You saw me kissing Mitzi?" Rudolph asked in a tone of stupefaction, "but how could you have?"

"I was in the woods at the *Linderhof*," Tilda answered.

"Good Lord!" he ejaculated. "Is there no end to your surprises, Tilda? How could I imagine that you would be in the woods?"

"I watched you and I wanted to know all about you," Tilda answered. "I thought perhaps you were a young married couple."

"Whatever you thought or did not think," Rudolph said firmly, "you will please forget all about it. At the same time, my precious one, I am glad you fell in love with me!"

"I thought you were the most exciting and – the most handsome man I had ever seen!"

She paused then went on,

"Obernia is full of handsome men. That *aide-de-camp*, the taller one, looks like a Greek God!"

"I shall dismiss him tomorrow!" Rudolph declared, "and replace him with someone old and white-haired."

Tilda gave a gurgle of laughter.

"I heard your uncle, the one with the white moustache, who is certainly old, say to someone,

'She is the prettiest little filly I have seen in years! Far too good for that young jackanapes, Maximilian. I have a good mind to have a go at her myself!'"

"Tilda!"

Rudolph's tone was shocked.

"That is my uncle Franz. He is a wicked old man and you are to have nothing to do with him, do you hear?"

"Your other uncle, the Archduke Karl, tickled the palm of my hand when he said goodbye."

Rudolph pulled her roughly against him.

"Let me make one thing clear, Tilda, I shall be a very jealous husband. If I catch you so much as looking at another man, I shall either murder or banish him. And beat you!"

"I think that would be – exciting!" Tilda said, cuddling a little closer. "It – thrills me when you are – strong and – masterful!"

Rudolph turned over on his side and looked down at her.

The fire gave a last dying effort to burn more brightly and the flames revealed Tilda's small flower-like face framed with her fair hair.

Her eyes were looking up at his and her lips were parted.

"You are so beautiful!" he said hoarsely, "so unbelievably beautiful. I adore you, but I have the feeling, my darling, that being married to you is going to be a worse torture than anything the Chinese ever devised."

"I want to make you – happy," Tilda whispered.

"And I want to make sure you belong to me," Rudolph answered. "I want you to love me and be quite certain that no other man can matter to you."

"I do love you!" Tilda said. "I did not know until now that the – world could hold so much – happiness and so much – love."

"That is what I wish you to feel," Rudolph said. "And I want you to want me as I want you, so that there can be no one else, now or ever!"

Tilda drew a deep breath.

"Make me – want you like – that," she whispered. "Please make me – want you, Rudolph!"

His mouth took possession of hers.

He felt her body move against him and knew that her heart was beating as wildly as his.

Then he swept her into a special Heaven for very naughty little angels who were utterly adorable and quite irresistible!

OTHER BOOKS IN THIS SERIES

The Barbara Cartland Eternal Collection is the unique opportunity to collect all five hundred of the timeless beautiful romantic novels written by the world's most celebrated and enduring romantic author.

Named the Eternal Collection because Barbara's inspiring stories of pure love, just the same as love itself, the books will be published on the internet at the rate of four titles per month until all five hundred are available.

The Eternal Collection, classic pure romance available worldwide for all time.

Made in the USA
Monee, IL
23 November 2020